Are You Gonna

Kiss Me or Not?

THOMPSON SQUARE

WITH TRAVIS THRASHER

HOWARD BOOKS

A Division of Simon & Schuster, Inc.

New York   Nashville   London   Toronto   Sydney   New Delhi

Howard Books
A Division of Simon & Schuster, Inc.
1230 Avenue of the Americas
New York, NY 10020

This book is a work of fiction. Any references to historical events, real people, or real places are used fictitiously. Other names, characters, places, and events are products of the author's imagination, and any resemblance to actual events or places or persons, living or dead, is entirely coincidental.

Story inspired by the musical composition "Are You Gonna Kiss Me or Not?" written by Jim Collins and David Lee Murphy, recorded by Thompson Square.

First Howard Books hardcover edition June 2013

HOWARD and colophon are trademarks of Simon & Schuster, Inc.

For information about special discounts for bulk purchases, please contact Simon & Schuster Special Sales at 1-866-506-1949 or business@simonandschuster.com.

The Simon & Schuster Speakers Bureau can bring authors to your live event. For more information or to book an event, contact the Simon & Schuster Speakers Bureau at 1-866-248-3049 or visit our website at www.simonspeakers.com.

Designed by Davina Mock-Maniscalco

Manufactured in the United States of America

10 9 8 7 6 5 4 3 2 1

Library of Congress Cataloging-in-Publication Data

Thompson Square (Musical group)
  Are you gonna kiss me or not? / Thompson Square, with Travis Thrasher.
    pages cm.
  1. Composers—Fiction. 2. Lyricists—Fiction. 3. Love stories. 4. Christian fiction. I. Thrasher, Travis, 1971- II. Title.
  PS3620.H689A89 2013
  813'.6—dc23
                              2012045185

ISBN 978-1-4516-9845-9
ISBN 978-1-4516-9846-6 (ebook)

Something happened the night you kissed me
My will to love was born again.
—Shelby Lynne, "I Need a Heart to Come Home To"

Oh and just one kiss
She'd fill them long summer nights with her tenderness.
—Bruce Springsteen, "She's the One"

Contents

Present Day

High School and the First Song
(1995–1996)

PRESENT DAY

HIGH SCHOOL AND THE ROOFTOP
(1996)

PRESENT DAY

COLLEGE AND DREAMS
(1996–1998)

PRESENT DAY

WEDDING BELLS
(2002)

PRESENT DAY

INTERSECTIONS
(2003–2005)

PRESENT DAY

FED UP AND BROKEN
(2008)

PRESENT DAY

CRISSCROSSING
(2009–2011)

PRESENT DAY

PRESENT DAY

Daniel in Distress

I ENTER THE ROOM to find this uncreative sack in a suit sitting there, and then I find myself thinking of Casey. This isn't unusual, since I do it all the time, but this is one of those moments I *really* wish she were here. I wish she were right next to me so we could be laughing about this in about an hour. I sorta know what's about to happen. I know that in just a few moments, I'm about to be let go as the head songwriter for *The Dandee Donuts* show.

Yeah, I know. There's a reason I haven't really told many people about my stint on *Dandee Donuts*. Most surely think Daniel has gone into hiding, playing his guitar and trying to finally make an album that would make the Boss smile. But no. Daniel is in isolation in Seattle, where the weather seems to match his mood.

This show makes *The Wiggles* look genius. No offense to *The Wiggles*. They really are a great show for kids, but I am not married and don't have any kids, and after working on *Dandee Donuts,* I don't want kids. I don't want them suckered by smiling corporate zombies like this one.

Daniel, have a seat, the rather soft handshake offers.

This guy's name is Stan Terma-something. I always think Terminal. Like terminal cancer. I know it's not Terminal, but I can't help thinking it. He's my boss's boss and only gets involved in meetings like this because my boss, Cynthia, is too weak to let anybody go or make any sort of decision.

"It's always a rather unfortunate part of my job to have meetings like this," Stan says to me. "We're all about 'rising up' around here."

I seriously want to throw up. He's using part of the marketing and sales copy for kids in this meeting. "Rise up with *Dandee Donuts* every morning at nine on the Sprout Channel!" Sometimes I hear that commercial in my sleep as I'm paddling down a jelly-filled river on my Long John.

Really, he's being merciful. This is like the guy coming up to the dying soldier and putting a bullet in his head.

"I spoke with Cynthia and I know she's informed you about our change of direction."

"I understand," I say.

It's strange, really.

I've got a stack of bills on my counter in the kitchen. And when I say stack, I mean a literal stack that can fall and decorate half the floor below. I'm behind in payments for a variety of reasons. I'm still getting paid, but this job hasn't paid the way I thought it would. My father's medical bills are really adding up, thanks to his awful insurance. And, well . . . the good old royalty checks haven't come in lately.

For a second I think of Dad, and what he might have said years ago when his mind was all there and he tried convincing me this music thing wasn't ever going to work.

Now it's time to settle down and get a job and act like a grown-up.

In many ways, I wish he could say those very things now. It would mean the man I grew up loving to hate was still around. The figure sitting in that reclining chair in our old house—that's not my father.

"You really have written some great songs."

I bet nobody ever said that to Paul McCartney or Bruce Springsteen in *that* particular type of tone. Like someone sipping a soda and saying, "This is really amazing soda" in a monotone and lifeless way.

This is strange because I find it refreshing. I want to start singing myself, even though it's been years since I finally accepted the fact that I'm not a very good singer.

"My kids still know all the lines to 'Bizarre Love Sprinkle'."

Trying to acquire the rights to do that song had been a nightmare, but coming up with lyrics for doughnuts arguing over what kind of sprinkles they wanted on top of New Order's "Bizarre Love Triangle" took perhaps fifteen minutes and a bottle of wine.

"I can only take half credit for that one," I say.

"It's just that—I know that Cynthia and you haven't been seeing eye-to-eye lately."

I smile. "Yeah."

"She told me about the argument in front of everybody."

I nod. "Yeah."

The meeting where I called her an absolute idiot and then proceeded to call her a few more things. This, of course, was after she rejected one of my songs by letting others make up her mind and convince her it didn't work.

It's a bit dark, someone said.

It's kinda sad, someone else said.

Doughnuts aren't sad, Cynthia said.

No, doughnuts are happy, someone else agreed.

I swear, if I have one more conversation about doughnuts, I'm going to go insane. I don't ever want to see another doughnut in my life.

"Do you have anything to say?" Stan the Terminal Man asked.

"Do you like what you do?"

The question came out of my mouth before I could stop it.

"Of course."

"No, I'm not asking whether you like being employed, or the fact that you have insurance and you get a check every other week. I'm not talking about how much you get paid and what you do and don't do and how many days you take off a year. I'm asking, do you *like* what you do? Did you dream of this when you were a kid?"

"Excuse me?"

Stan's attitude suddenly seems a bit more serious and stern. Maybe I've finally wakened this vampire from his eternal slumber.

"I'm not trying to be a pain in the butt," I say. "Really. I just want an honest answer."

"I've worked very hard to make this company what it is today, and I'm proud of the work we do. So yes, I love my job and love what it stands for and what we create."

I think of that news report the other day that said something like half of the population is obese.

That's what you create from this show. Happy little kids who keep munching, and then one day, they're fifty years old but the munching hasn't stopped and they no longer feel so Dandee.

I look him in the eyes, and it appears he's not lying.

Along with sipping the Kool-Aid, he's managed to eat the Dandee Donuts as well.

"I think it's time to just call it a day," Stan says to me. "Don't you think?"

He's talking down to me even though he's really not that much older than I am.

I nod and stand up and shake that doughy hand again.

I bet he's got cream filling in his soul.

See, this is the sort of thing that has happened to me. Every thought has a doughnut analogy.

I leave his office and close the door behind me.

I'm thirty-five years old, and the dream is officially over.

BRUCE REMINDS ME of what I really wanted to do later that night as I work my way through a six-pack of cheap beer and listen to *Born to Run*. This album always reminds me of my youth, when I discovered Springsteen and figured out what I wanted to do. I wanted to do *that*. I wanted to make soulful songs that stirred the heart and told stories. I wanted to be real. I wanted people to hear the sweat coming off those melodies.

Dad wanted me to be like my older brothers and excel in sports. But I couldn't throw a football like Philip or hit a baseball like Jeff.

I wanted to follow my dreams, and that's exactly what I did. Yet those dreams brought me here, to stale-doughnut land.

Yeah, I can hear you, you ghost and you demon and you angel all tied into one.

Casey knows about these dreams. We talked a lot about them. We even made a promise about them once.

I need to tell her. I need to finally tell her I can't hold up my end of our deal.

Not that she wants to hear from me. Like, ever again. She's moved on with her life and that's what I should be doing with mine.

But if this is moving on, then, man, I cannot wait to see what my fortieth birthday holds for me, right, Case?

I'm talking to an imaginary Casey in my mind while I'm drinking bad beer and being reminded of real rock and roll.

I never thought I'd be such an awful failure at thirty-five. I want to say it is what it is, but I hate that saying. It *was* what it was, but right now, this moment, this very second that I'm thinking of Casey, really hurts.

Call Gary tomorrow and see if he has any kind of answer.

This thought is depressing, since Gary Mains is my manager in Nashville. My quasi-manager, to be honest, since I haven't sold a song in years. I've been waiting for a follow-up call or e-mail from him since I sent him a CD of demo songs a few months ago.

When someone doesn't call or e-mail after a few months, you know what the answer is.

There comes a point when everybody has to grow up and realize the dream isn't going to happen. When the silence and the dim light of the room aren't just a snapshot of your evening, but of your life. When the music doesn't matter anymore and the words are no longer there. When you realize the world isn't listening and maybe never listened to begin with.

If it's really over, I need to tell her. I need to let her know that I broke the promise, that I broke our promise.

It's been two years since I saw her. That doesn't matter. I don't know exactly where she is or what she's doing, but that doesn't matter either.

I need to tell her the dream is over. I need to give back a portion of my promise.

Maybe she can find something to do with it.

I've held it for long enough and it's only brought me to this sad, sappy point.

Enough.

I get out a notebook and start writing a letter. I don't know any other way to get in touch with her. I'd text her if I had her number, but she changed that a long time ago. She's not a social-network sort of gal, at least judging from the last few hundred times I searched for her on the Internet like a weirdo stalker boy. This is all I can do, this pen-to-paper sort of old-fashioned thing. I know her mother still lives in their house in Asheville, North Carolina. And last I checked, the post office still delivered letters.

After an hour and another Springsteen album and a few more beers, I've got a doozy of a letter. I've thought about telling her everything, but instead I simply say the following:

> *Dear Casey:*
> *Are you gonna kiss me or not?*
> *Daniel*

I fold it up and find an envelope and seal it. I'll find the address of her mother tomorrow and will send it out.

This letter says everything I need to say. It says more than I ever could.

This is our history and our story, summed up by seven simple words.

Casey Comes 'Round

SOMETIMES I WISH love were as easy as a three-minute song. You have the tension and the drama and the angst resolve itself into a beautiful chorus everybody can hum and remember and sing along to at a wedding. But songs and weddings are just the start. It's the silent days long after the music has stopped playing where love is made or broken.

I turn off the car and can feel the hush wrap around me like the thick Georgia humidity outside. I didn't expect to be here today. I didn't expect to be facing the four sets of double doors all staring down at me like the Supreme Court, waiting to issue out some verdict on my life. My car is the only one parked in the long, circular driveway, yet I know I'm not the only one here, at this estate home on this sprawling corner lot alongside some swanky golf course.

One of those doors opens before I can even climb out of my car. I see him standing there, still handsome and still looking straight through me like he always could. No matter how much time passes, he still makes me feel this way inside. Jerked forward, like someone grabbing my hand and leading me onto a dance floor even when they know I'm the world's worst dancer. That would all be fine if the person pulling actually wanted to dance with me, but he simply wants to look good on the dance floor.

I remain silent until I'm standing before the wide steps leading to a wider porch. "Hi, Burke."

"I didn't think you'd come."

"I didn't either."

He looks thinner than the last time I saw him. His skin a bit too pale, a bit too yellowish. Up close, he's a gaunt shadow of the Burke Bennett I married.

"Did you find it okay?"

"This is probably the only Peachtree Plantation around."

He smiles at my comment. "I meant once you got through the gates. I always seem to get turned around."

"I'm here." Even after promising myself never to be here again. "Still looks as new as it looked five years ago."

"I think it looks even more new now than when Dad was living in it. Would you like to come in?"

Burke is being polite, which is a big step for him. Respect was one of the first things to go in our marriage.

"Well, we could just stand out here and melt."

"Temperature's awful, isn't it?" he replies, set at ease by my joke. "How was your drive?"

"It was fine."

"I told you—I would've paid for a plane ticket."

"It took five hours. To fly would've taken the same amount of time."

Burke leads me into the great room, which looks massive and clean and unlived-in. I hear our footsteps tap on the wooden floor. The room is surrounded by windows letting in the afternoon sun. There's a piano in the corner that has a framed picture of Burke's father resting on top of it.

"My aunt put that there. For visitors. It's a good picture of him, isn't it? It's rare to see my father smiling."

"I'm so sorry," I say.

He knows what I'm talking about and only nods. For a moment, we're not sure what to do. You can give your heart and soul and body to a man, but when you finally sign those divorce papers, a simple greeting can suddenly seem difficult. We eventually hug each other in a gesture both familiar and awkward at the same moment.

"You look beautiful, Casey."

"I look old."

I'm wearing a summer dress with sandals. I didn't want to dress up for Burke, but I didn't exactly want to look like I'd thrown in the towel since we separated. I realized I was way overthinking what I was going to wear, so I decided on this understated and simple number.

Burke shakes his head at my comment and looks at me in a weird way. Not creepy weird, but weird because I don't recognize this look. "You look beautiful," he says again.

I can't help but brush my hair back and look away. There might be ten thousand ways to describe a woman, yet he uses the same simple word. Twice. Not because he doesn't mean it, but just because he doesn't have the depth to think of something more creative.

And how many women has he said that to?

"Come on. Let me get you something to drink." He begins to walk over to the adjoining kitchen.

"A water is fine."

He looks back as he opens the stainless-steel refrigerator. "Sure you don't want anything stronger?"

I nod and give him a polite smile. "Around you? A water will be just fine."

He laughs. "I've missed that, you know."

"My charm?"

"Yeah. Your charm."

He doesn't say anything more because we've already said all there is to say. The words won't ever leave us either. They are carved out on our souls, and no apology or counseling session will ever be able to smooth them over. There were plenty of both while we were married.

Burke hands me the water and gives me a long and hard look.

"What?" I ask as I see his lips begin to form a smile.

"I can see how you charmed my father. It's not surprising, especially knowing Dad."

"Your father barely knew me."

Burke laughs. "Yeah. And that's why. He didn't realize someone so cute could be so . . ."

"So what?"

"So Casey-like."

"Be nice," I tell him. "I just got here."

"I know. I don't want you to leave this house like you did last time."

I nod, but the memory is a painful one. Burke knows that perhaps his last comment wasn't the best thing he could have said. But that's Burke, and that's the story of our relationship.

"Look—let me go to the office and grab you a copy of the will."

This is why I'm here.

According to Burke, this five-thousand-square-foot-home, worth well over a million dollars, is half mine. This is what he explained to me over the phone after several attempts to contact me. I thought he was drunk and lying, but he confirmed it after a few more conversations.

I still find the whole thing unbelievable. A part of me hopes it's all some kind of ruse to get me to see him again. That would be less complicated. But nothing about Burke and me has ever been simple.

★ ★ ★

"LOOK, I'M NOT even going to try and hide this."

Burke has entered the kitchen with a folder and a bottle that I first think must be some kind of red wine. He puts the bottle on the counter and I notice the old scary-looking man on the label, as well as the words "malt scotch whisky." Burke looks through a couple of cabinets before finding some glasses. He puts one in front of me and I seem to lean back, as if smelling something vile.

"Dad used to tell me about buying this years ago," Burke says, the far-off and wild look in his eyes, the one that used to frighten me a bit. "'A 1955 Glenfarclas, fifty years old.' He'd talk about it like it was the son he always dreamed of having. I mean—it was whisky. Bought it in 2005. He'd bring it up every time I was around him. Telling me the story of it like it's some kind of person or something."

Burke curses as he opens the bottle. I watch Burke pour the dark liquid into two small glasses.

"The last week, I've been finding myself wanting to do every single thing that monster told me never to do. I've been waiting to open this for a while. Having you back here certainly seems like the right occasion."

"When did you start drinking scotch?" I ask as the glass he poured for me remains on the counter.

Burke laughs and curses. "That's the thing—I don't drink scotch. You know how much this bottle cost? Over ten grand. Can you believe that? He bought it in 2005 for ten thousand dollars. I mean—that's obscene. Just like Pop. Just like our wonderful family. Just like me."

The curse he lets out still unnerves me a bit and makes me shudder. It's not the words themselves. I've never been a big fan of cursing, but it's the anger behind those words uttered by my ex that bothers me.

I remember that anger very well. The combination of alcohol and anger and creative adjectives coming out of Burke's mouth was a mixture a bit too strong for me to take.

He holds his glass up, smiles, and then stares out the wall of windows to the west. "Hope you're watching, Pop."

As he puts down his glass next to my full one, Burke must see the look on my face.

"I'm sorry," he says. "Look, I just—"

"Lost your father," I interrupt. "You don't have to explain. I understand."

"Yeah. Casey understands. The one person in my life and in the South who understands anything to do with the Bennett family."

"Just because I understand doesn't mean I'm going to stand here and watch you go off the rails."

"No, please—that's not what this is about. I'm not going to. I'm fine. Trust me, Casey. I'm fine. Things are going really good."

Burke takes the other glass and pours it out in the sink, then places the bottle over on the side of the counter like a bottle of soda.

"I think that stuff is *way* overpriced," Burke says.

"I would have been here at the funeral if I knew it wouldn't have caused a scene."

"You should have been there when we met with the lawyer."

"Was there a reading of the will?"

"No—they don't do stuff like that. At least I don't think they do. The lawyer met with us to discuss our father's will. As you can imagine, little baby sister had a major meltdown."

"How is Bridgett?"

He curses again, this time in describing his sister. "She's exactly the person Mom and Dad created her to be."

Bridgett is the one who would have made life miserable for me if I had attended the funeral a week ago. Back when I was still married to Burke, when I last saw the whole family during the nightmarish funeral for their mother, Bridgett threatened to kill me. There was a part of her drunken and drug-fueled outburst that made me think she wasn't lying.

Now I understand a little better why she had lashed out at me. It wasn't because Burke and I were getting a divorce. It was because I was the woman her father wished she could be.

"She still thinks the will is invalid. She's threatening to sue. I told her to sue Dad. It's not my fault he left the house to you and me."

The way he says that, as simple as saying peanut-butter-and-jelly sandwich, is a bit surreal.

"*I* still think the will is invalid," I say. "Your father knew we were divorced, right?"

I'm being facetious. Yet there's no way this house can in any way be mine.

Burke opens the folder and produces a page. He reads off some legalese that mentions my name.

"'This gift is distributable to Casey May Sparkland whether or not she is married to my son, Burke James Bennett, at the time of my passing.' The gift he's talking about is this house and this lot and basically everything in this house."

"And what about Bridgett?"

"Oh, she got stuff. She's fine. She's got plenty to support her expensive habits until she dies."

Anybody else might be surprised by Burke's harshness, but he hasn't even started. Nothing fuels his deep-rooted anger more than his hatred toward his family. I know, because I was once family.

"I can't take anything from your father," I blurt out, making it clear right away where I'm coming from.

There is no discussion to be had. Whatever was given to me by Burke's father is Burke's to have. Plain and simple. I made that choice the moment we divorced.

"Okay, sign here then," Burke says, handing me the sheet of paper, then laughing.

"Are you kidding?"

"Yes, I'm kidding. Jeez. Can you just relax and stay for longer than ten minutes?"

"I'm expecting Bridgett to come through that door any minute," I say, only partially joking.

"Thank God Dad didn't give her the guns."

The joke makes me laugh. I don't want to, but I realize how worried I've been about seeing Burke again. I didn't want to come down here and I didn't want to see him again. I especially didn't want to have to discuss being mentioned in a family will when I'm no longer part of that family.

Then again, there are lots of things about my life I haven't wanted. But you don't always get the things you want the most. That's what I've learned the older I become.

Burke comes up and puts his hands on my shoulders. "Look— let's just—let me show you the back porch. Let's have some lemonade. Sit on the porch and just chill."

His touch still feels familiar, just like his voice and his eyes and his smile. They're deadly and dangerous and there's no way they're going to fool me again. Yet I'm tired and I don't want to leave. I can't leave. There's too much to talk about related to his father's passing and my name being mentioned in the will.

"Okay," I say. "But just for a short while."

Just until we both agree what we'll do about everything. Then I'll go and leave Burke to this life I no longer have a place in. I'll leave and go back home and continue to try to find the life I'm supposed to have now. Whatever it might be.

THE FIRST TIME I visited Burke's family, they lived in an old Southern mansion that had been in the family since the Civil War era. The house sat on a huge plot of land about fifteen minutes outside of Savannah. I remember being there for a few minutes and making a *Gone With The Wind* joke that completely went over Burke's head. I thought it was just him being a jock.

I'd eventually learn he was a lot more old-school-money snob than dumb jock.

A jock who comes from old money? Watch out.

The mansion was always the subject of some great big drama in the Bennett family. Charles Bennett, Burke's father, was the eldest of five, and the house didn't belong to just him. It was falling apart and required a lot of money for upkeep. The siblings loved to get together during the holidays and drink enough to summon up the courage to fight about the mansion. One wanted to keep it, another wanted it leveled, another wanted it fixed up. Charles Bennett had to navigate through these waters, but he was the most stubborn one of all, trying to keep the house at all costs.

Eventually, a fire made the decision for all of them. It happened after Burke and I had been married a couple of years. I was sad to see it happen because he had proposed to me on those house grounds. Perhaps that should have served as an omen. Charles certainly believed it was no accident and ended up severing his ties with his two brothers and two sisters because he didn't trust any of them.

I want to ask Burke which of them showed up for the funeral. I'm guessing most of them showed up, but it had to be sad and awkward to say the least.

"Here," Burke says as he offers me a glass of lemonade on one of the back porches of the house. "I promise there's no thousand-dollar shot of whisky in there."

"I was really hoping for one." I take it as he sits down on the white rocking chair that matches the one I'm already comfortable in. Steps roll off this porch and onto a small stone sidewalk that weaves its way through oak trees and lawn to a small pond.

"Pretty, huh?" Burke says. "You know—Mom was already pretty sick by the time they moved here. She was upstairs in her bed most of the time. My dad—I swear he spent most of his time in the office on the main floor, the one we just passed. I don't know if either of them ever even stepped foot back here."

"It's a shame."

"Yeah."

I can hear the constant buzzing in the background. "Are those cicadas?"

Burke shakes his head. "No. They came a couple of years ago. They pop up every thirteen years. They were brutal. No, those are just some katydids starting up early. You know what they sound like at night. Last I checked, Asheville still had katydids and grasshoppers."

"Oh, you didn't hear? Asheville's really changing. Since it's becoming a lot more artsy, the katydids and other tree dwellers have decided to go somewhere else. They need to be around true rednecks."

"Then this isn't the place for them," Burke says. "I swear—you'd think we're in the Hamptons or somewhere like that."

"I've never been to the Hamptons."

"Somewhere where rich folks act like rich folks. There's a yacht club and a country club and a golf club and an old-rich-farts club."

"How old do you have to be to join that?" I joke.

"Ancient. Like ninety or something."

I take a sip of the lemonade and am not sure what to say. I've always been good at speaking my mind—so everybody's always told me—and I've always told this man next to me exactly what I was thinking. Exactly what I was thinking and usually exactly when I was thinking it. But now I don't know what to say. I want to be civil and I'm fine to continue to just talk this way, but I'm here to figure out what to do about the will.

"Are you teaching any this summer?" Burke asks.

"I'm just doing a little tutoring. I figured I'd take the summer off."

I don't finish my sentence.

To work on my writing.

That's what I'd tell him if I could talk about that sort of stuff. But he used to always make fun of my love of poetry. It was one of the many things he never understood about me.

"How about you?"

"Yeah, I'm taking the summer off too."

Now I'm not even sure if he's joking. "Are you still running your father's business?"

"Yeah," Burke says in a casual manner. "I'm just taking over where he left off. Doing nothing. He's done nothing and made a nice living at it."

I'm sure Burke is doing a little more than "nothing" for the finance company his father started over a dozen years ago, right after Burke and I married.

"I still don't understand why he put me in the will."

"Seriously? What about it don't you get?"

I shrug and continue looking out beyond the trees and the golf fairway to the right of this porch.

"Your father has always been so loyal to 'the family.' To the Bennett family. He was the one who refused to give up the family mansion until it finally burned to the ground."

"Yeah, until someone torched it."

"You still believe that?"

"Yep."

"Why, if he's such a family guy, does he put my name in the will?"

Burke crosses his legs and leans over toward me. "My father has been in love with you since the moment I brought you to meet them. You used to make him laugh."

"Because I could be so dense."

"No, it's not because of that. I mean, yes, you *can* be dense."

"Watch it," I say with a grin.

"You were this fresh breeze that came blowing into this stale life of his. That old house really just represented Dad. Charles Bennett. A part of him died when it burned down. And you know—I'm not gonna say this to make you feel bad. But a part of him also died when we got divorced."

Something blows through me and urges me to be defensive. Yet I pause for a moment, knowing Burke isn't trying to get at me. I know he's just telling the truth.

"That's why I wanted—why I needed—you to come down here," Burke continues. "Because I need you to know some things. Not just about this place but about me."

I wipe the beads of sweat off my forehead. The day is getting cooler but it's still heavy with humidity.

Yeah, and heavy with memories.

"I've changed."

Burke says this in a tone that is very un-Burke-ish. Not demanding and not entitled and not arrogant. He says it in a very quiet and humble manner.

"I know you might not believe me, but I have," he says. "And Casey—I want you back. I made a big mistake."

A part of me wants to remind him what I once told him. But I hold my tongue. I keep from telling him he made many mistakes, not just one.

"I know what you're thinking and I know you told me so. But I was stupid. I was still searching. I didn't know what I wanted."

"I didn't either."

"Are you kidding?" Burke says, looking down at me with that square face of his. "You've always known what you wanted."

This is part of the problem. Even now, after all this time, after all the things I said and tried to do, he still doesn't get it. He still doesn't know the me who never even began to get what she wanted.

Stay unemotional. Stay cool and calm. Stay focused.

"I think a lot of the things *I* wanted were things my parents wanted," I say. "The whole wonderful plan, just like they had.

Going to Duke. Studying *literature*. Staying in school to earn a bunch of degrees instead of actually writing."

"How's your family?"

"They're doing well. My parents are still competing for all the girls' love and attention. My father remarried. All my sisters are having babies. Mom is into some New Age thing. She still always asks about you, by the way. Every day is an adventure."

He reaches over and takes my lemonade and then puts it down. Then he holds my hands in his.

There was a time in my life when Burke Bennett standing there holding my hands and looking into my eyes would have made my knees buckle and my hands shake. Not in the clichéd sort of romance-novel way but literally. He was so fine to look at, this solid structure in front of me. But that time feels like another world, another woman.

"I want more adventures in my life," he says.

"Going over the falls isn't an adventure," I say rather quickly. "And it sure isn't fun."

"Then we won't go over the falls. We'll stay out of the water."

"We already did. We can't hike back up that mountain."

"Says who?"

I never expected to come out here for this. Four years and suddenly he wants me back?

"Burke—I'm sorry about your father."

"I'm not talking about him. I'm talking about me. About us. Have you—is there someone else?"

"Yeah," I say in disbelief. "I eloped this past weekend to Vegas. We adopted a trio of boys too."

"I'm just asking."

"You told me you fell out of love. The way you might fall out of a plane."

"I didn't mean it."

I back up and face him so I can look at him without him touching me. "You meant every word you said. Don't back-track."

"I regret saying them."

"I regret you saying them too. I regret a lot of the stuff you did. But it's done. We're done."

"I just want to wash it all away. Wipe the slate clean. Just start over. Redo."

I let out a nervous sigh. "You might be able to do that. But *we* can't do that."

"This place would be a pretty nice place to start over."

"Maybe this has all been a big mistake." I stand up and move toward the edge of the porch.

For a moment I don't move or say another word. I'm starting to think I should walk away and leave this place.

"Please, just. Don't leave, Casey. Please."

"But I can't just—"

"Just—just stay. For dinner, okay? For an easy and uncompli-cated dinner. I have enough food in the kitchen to feed a hundred people. Please. Just—don't leave. Not like this. Everybody else is gone."

I pause for a moment, then remind myself why I'm here.

"What do I have to do to take care of the will?" I ask him.

His dark eyes focus on me for a moment. "We'll go see my lawyer. He'll take care of the details. All I ask is for you to consider—just consider—what life might be like with me back in it."

Once again, I'm speechless. I don't know what to say. I don't know where to begin.

"It's not like I'm expecting you to get your belongings and move in here," he says. "It's just—it's complicated and we have to figure out what to do. So don't just—don't freak out and drive off and never call me again. Please. This could really be a good thing. For both of us."

I nod. I can't help but nod. I want to help him out, even though I should really and truly be taking the knife and plunging it into his heart the same way he plunged it into mine. But I can't do that. Not to someone I once loved.

"Come on—let's go back inside," Burke says. "I can show you the will and have you read it over if you want. Or I can show you around the house. Maybe you'll reconsider once you see just how nice everything is."

Burke smiles. Even now, after all this time, he has an ability to get his way. We both know it and that's the way things have always been.

But things are different now. I won't tell him how, but they're different.

The world has changed for me. If only I could have seen the colors change years ago.

When your heart is broken once, it has the ability to heal. But when it's broken twice, it vows to never allow it to happen again.

I wish he could know that. Not the man standing here in front of me, but the man who taught me this. The man who broke my heart both times.

Everything has an answer
But you're a question waiting to be found
Something so simple and curious
An equation that makes the world go 'round
So complex and intricate
An infinite number going on
We celebrate the mystery that's you
By writing you this Pi song

—Sparkland & Winter, "The Pi Song" (never officially recorded)

HIGH SCHOOL AND

THE FIRST SONG

(1995–1996)

Cuts Like a Knife

O N THE FIRST day of his last year of high school, Daniel Winter noticed Casey Sparkland. It didn't matter that they had already spent three years together in these halls and classrooms. Most of the time, he was thinking about football and rock and roll. Probably not in that order. Yet between second and third periods on that Monday morning, Daniel took a second glance at someone and didn't take his eyes off her.

"Who is that?" he asked Teddy.

"Who? Oh, you talking about Casey?"

He knew Casey, of course, yet Daniel had never noticed this girl he'd grown up around. Not like this. Not in a way where everything else suddenly disappeared. *That's not Casey.*

"What about her?" his friend asked.

Teddy probably would miss a Victoria's Secret model walking past them. It wasn't that he didn't find a hot girl hot, but he just was oblivious because they never paid him any attention. When every girl you'd ever known called you Teddy Bear, well, you probably wouldn't bother looking at them in any sort of romantic way.

"That's Casey Sparkland?"

Even though Daniel didn't really know her, he knew her last name. Everybody knew a last name like that. And everybody knew Casey as well. Chatty, friendly, well-to-do, Liam Carter-loving Casey.

"Yeah," Teddy said. "Talking, as usual."

"What happened to her?"

The big guy was thumbing through a music magazine, but his round eyes suddenly looked up. "What do you mean?"

"I mean, look at her."

Teddy stared but obviously didn't see the startling difference Daniel was talking about.

"She's like . . ." Daniel couldn't finish the statement.

He was about to say that Casey Sparkland was kinda hot, and she was, not that Teddy would even care. This was strange. The Casey he knew was the one to speak up first in class, the kind usually leading the charge for some kind of school thing, the outgoing girl always voted onto the Homecoming Court because everybody liked her. Everybody *had* to like Casey.

She was also practically married to Liam Carter, though Liam was nowhere to be found on this day.

Something about Casey was different. As if the summer had changed her in some way. It wasn't just the tiny skirt she was wearing. It was just her whole vibe.

It had been a long, boring summer, and for the first time in a long time, Daniel suddenly felt curious and interested. He couldn't help doing something he'd never done in his entire history at T. C. Roberson High.

He proceeded to go over and talk with Casey.

"HI."

"Oh come on," Casey said in an exasperated tone.

"What?"

She brushed back long, strawberry blond hair that seemed lighter than Daniel remembered. Her eyes glared at him.

This wasn't quite the response he expected.

"Okay, go on," Casey said. "Get it out of your system."

Daniel already regretted this. He shook his head and laughed. "I'm missing something."

Up close, he noticed the sprinkling of freckles across her cheeks and nose. Casey wasn't very tall, but straightened herself as if she were meeting the Queen of England. "Hello, Daniel Winter."

"Hello," he said slowly, feeling amused and bewildered at the same time.

"So just tell me. When was the last time you came up to me and said hi with that Daniel Winter charm?"

Oh boy.

Even if he didn't know her that well, Daniel knew that type of tone in a girl. It was the kind that made guys search for the nearest exit and take off down the road as fast as they could.

"Charm? There's nothing charming about the way I say hi."

"When was it?" she asked.

That wasn't a question. That was a demand.

"I don't know," he said, totally baffled at this conversation.

"I know. It was sophomore year."

Daniel laughed. "Is a 'hi' such a bad thing?"

"Sure it is. When you haven't gotten a single hi for years and then it suddenly comes when you wear a skirt and a top like this."

"You say that like you're being forced to wear it."

Casey shook her head in disgust. "You think these belong to me?"

Now Daniel was really lost. "You're, uh, wearing 'em, so . . ."

"It was a bet. A bet I lost."

"Oh." For a moment, Daniel looked around to see if anybody was watching this bizarre exchange. Casey wasn't the quietest girl in the school, so her voice could carry. All the way to Texas.

She seemed to suddenly come to the conclusion why he had approached her. Her face looked in disbelief as she burst out in laughter. Mocking laughter.

"You actually *like* what I'm wearing?"

Daniel wasn't sure how to answer that question.

Is it wrong to like your outfit?

Daniel sighed and shook his head and raised his hands in defeat. "I'm not quite sure what I did here."

Suddenly, Daniel's first day back at T. C. Roberson was becoming a drag.

"You know that Liam and I broke up?" Casey asked.

"How would I know?" Daniel asked. "I mean, you two are usually joined at the hip."

"We've never been joined at the hip."

"You sorta have been since, what—junior high?"

"Sophomore year," she interjected.

Daniel laughed. "Okay . . . time-out. Look, Casey—sorry for the friendly chat. I was just—"

"What was your end goal here?"

Daniel paused for a moment, glancing at her blue eyes. Even though she was getting all over him for some unknown reason, he liked looking her dead in the eyes. Especially when she appeared a little upset or irked or whatever was happening with Casey at the moment.

Her eyes actually made him feel a bit nervous. Which was crazy, because he never got nervous around girls. Ever. Except for right at that very moment.

"Look—I didn't really—it wasn't like there was some sort of 'end goal,' whatever that might be."

"Just tell me," Casey demanded.

Daniel glanced around again, and this time, yeah, there were some onlookers.

Suddenly he felt a fire inside of him. He didn't deserve this lashing out from someone he didn't even know.

"Actually, to be honest, you're all I can think about," he said with a grin on his face.

"You're a jerk."

"I've been called worse."

"Seriously—you really think this is me?" She pointed at her outfit.

"I thought it looked nice. Until you suddenly turned into Possessed Girl or something like that."

"'Nice'," she repeated in an astonished tone. "And you thought, what? I'd suddenly swoon for the football player in a rock band?"

"You forgot to mention my wonderful dimple."

"Guys are all the same."

"I was actually just trying to hook you up with Teddy," Daniel said, no longer interested in being serious anymore.

"He's funny and sweet. You only think you are, and you play a guitar."

The moment Casey said "guitar," he could see it. A little light in her eyes that gave her away. Not a fighting torch but something that resembled her last name. A spark. A playful little light.

Is she the one joking now?

"So playing the guitar is a bad thing?"

"That means you want to go on and be a rock star and sing songs and be *that* kind of guy. Unless you go to play football, which I doubt will happen. I've seen you play."

Daniel let out a loud laugh. This was crazy.

As he looked around, Daniel discovered they were now the only two people standing in the hallway. Somehow the bell had already rung but he hadn't heard it. Daniel was sure Ms. Sparkles there would simply get a nice little wink when she walked into her class late. Daniel would get a lecture like he always did.

"I didn't expect a simple 'hi' would end up with someone bashing my football skills."

"I'm being kind. I could have commented on your singing."

Daniel almost choked in surprise. Suddenly he hated this girl with more energy and passion than he'd felt all summer long.

"You know—I'm truly sorry for suddenly noticing you and thinking you might be nice," he said.

"I've been nice for a long time."

"Are you saying I haven't?"

Casey glared at him. "Uh, several of my friends would probably say otherwise."

Oh, yeah, that's right.

"And Daniel—those same girls *loved* you. Plural. That's a big plural. I've had one guy in my life tell me he loved me, and that recently ended really badly."

"Okay."

"Truth hurts, huh?"

Daniel stood there, amazed. No girl in his entire seventeen years had ever spoken to him like this. Even the ones he'd broken up with. Casey seemed to notice the expression on his face. For a moment, they stared at each other. Daniel gave her a polite nod, then walked politely back out of her life, never expecting to step foot in it again.

Someone Else's Dream

*I*T STILL FELT strange to know her dad wasn't coming home anymore. At least, not to stay.

Casey parked the Land Rover on the side of the circling driveway and she and Brittany climbed out. Their house in Biltmore Forest was on a winding road stuck in the middle of dense woods. They were on a hill that overlooked the golf course her father had loved to play on. Casey had never really enjoyed playing, but her younger sisters did. She wondered if things would have been different if she had been a son. Something told her she would be spending a lot more time around the country club.

Brittany was in her own world that afternoon, which was fine because Casey hadn't felt like talking about the first day back at school with anybody, especially her younger sister. She had seen Liam a couple times, and both times she had felt awkward around him. All because of the outfit. The ridiculous outfit. Brittany had even made a comment about it that morning on the way to school, but Casey had told her she wouldn't drive her home if she kept that up.

She followed Brittany into the house and then picked up her sister's backpack to put it in the entryway near the garage. Her mom had picked up Emily and Ashley from middle school in the afternoon while Casey was starting to drive her father's old Land Rover. "Old" meant it was a couple of years old.

He had replaced his "old" SUV with something new and sleek and sexy, like many things. Like the convertible. Like the town house on the lake. And like the girl only nine years older than Casey. A girl who had surely caught her father's attention by wearing something like she was wearing.

What was I thinking?

She finally felt a little better—just a little—once she was in a pair of jeans and a Duke sweatshirt. Both of her parents had attended Duke University, so she had lots and lots of Duke apparel to choose from. With her door shut to make sure one of her sisters didn't barge into her room, Casey thought of the miserable first day of school.

All she had wanted to do was punch something, and suddenly out of the blue—no, not out of the blue, but out of nowhere— came smiling, smirking Daniel Winter with his smooth talk. In that moment, her fellow senior became a walking and talking punching bag. Casey let go.

Of course, it had nothing to do with Daniel. It had everything to do with Liam. Well, mostly Liam, and then Liam's new little flame, the sophomore tramp named Violet who had captured his eye at a party while Casey was spending a week with her sisters and mom and grandparents at Myrtle Beach. By the time she got back, Violet had captured his heart, too, assuming he actually had one. For the rest of the summer, the two had been a pair, and Casey had dreaded seeing them when school started.

Perhaps a small and leftover amount of anger could be directed at her best friend, Alison, who had the bright idea for her to get Liam's attention on the first day of school by wearing "something sexy."

The idea backfired, of course, when Liam saw her and laughed out loud while walking down the hall with his new girlfriend.

Then, to make matters worse, Daniel showed up out of the blue to talk to her.

Now she not only felt moronic for trying to impress someone not worth her time and effort, but she had run over a guy she barely knew.

She didn't really know Daniel Winter at all. Insulting his football playing wasn't a slam. He barely played, and he always seemed like it was just something he had been forced to do. Daniel was a musician and acted like one. Even earlier that afternoon, he'd been wearing a Bryan Adams T-shirt and faded jeans. He wasn't a jock. He was a rocker.

Casey tried to forget about the day by slipping in the newest

CD she'd bought. She went to the second track and cranked "Let's Go to Vegas." For a moment, she looked at the beautiful woman on the cover and wished she could be as attractive and happy as Faith Hill looked. Maybe one day. Maybe when she was older and didn't have any Liams in her life.

By the time track three came around and the tempo slowed down, her mood began to shift again.

The first night of the school year and she was already dreading the rest of it. So far, so much of her time in high school had been spent with Liam. She never wondered what life after high school would be like, because she always assumed Liam would be a part of it. They had been together a couple of years, and they were both planning on going to Duke.

Guys are all the same.

This was a cliché, but it was one Casey was starting to believe.

All guys, including Mr. Smiley Rocker Wannabe.

She cranked the music and decided not to think about all of this anymore for the night.

CASEY AND HER sisters were watching *Melrose Place* when her mother said she had a call. She said it in the way that made her think it was Liam.

She grabbed the cordless from her mom and went into the great room at the front of the house. Her mind was full of a thousand things she wanted and needed to say to Liam. Questions. Answers. Demands.

"Hi, Casey?"

Liam sounded sick. His voice was lower, more subdued.

"Yeah?"

"It's Daniel. Daniel Winter."

She didn't say a word. Her heart was racing because she was expecting a male voice, but not *this* male voice.

Not again.

"Hello?" he asked.

"Yeah."

"Hey, I hope I'm not bothering you."

"I was just watching a show."

"What are you watching?"

"Melrose Place," Casey said without thinking.

"Are you serious?"

She detected that attitude, the one she knew about, the Daniel Winter cooler-than-everybody vibe.

"It's a great show," she said. She did not fully believe this, but was not about to back down.

"Um, okay."

"Did you call for a reason?"

"Yeah, look—I just—I wasn't exactly sure what happened or what I did today, you know."

Now's the time to apologize for lashing out at this guy.

"I mean, I've never even spoken with you," Daniel said.

"Yeah, that's my point," she said, thinking of that outfit again.

Thinking of the miniskirt made her think of Liam, then of Violet, then of her father, then of all the men in the world and what boneheads they all were.

"I wasn't trying to be rude. I just thought you looked nice, like some girl visiting our school from New York or some big, fashionable city." He paused, then added, "I thought you looked really pretty."

Daniel Winter could have said a lot of things, but she wasn't expecting him to say that. He didn't say she looked hot, or stunning, or good. He said that about the fashion bit, then followed it up saying something that felt charming and authentic.

She was glad she was on the phone, because if he could have seen her, he would have seen her blushing.

I'm just Casey who has a mound of reddish-blond curly fries for hair and has never met a sentence she didn't fail to utter.

"Hello?" he asked.

"I'm sorry. That was just a very nice thing to say."

"I can be a nice guy, you know."

Don't believe him. That's what they all say.

"Look—I sorta feel bad about today," she said.

"You sure about that?" he asked.

"What?"

"Well, you *sorta* feel bad. So that's a little guilt, but not a lot."

"What do you mean?" Casey asked, not following him.

"I mean—my pride was really hurt today. I might not be able to get over it."

Now he was teasing her.

"I think you'll be fine," Casey told him.

"I think I need to make up for ignoring you all these years," Daniel said. "For never bothering to talk with you before."

He's still trying to hit on me.

She laughed for the first time, which was rare because she usually laughed a lot. "Yeah, right."

"Seriously."

"Stop it," she said, assuming he was joking.

"No, I'm being serious."

"Okay."

"So you sorta feel bad and I want to, uh, correct things."

"How?"

"By seeing if you'd let me ask you out."

Suddenly the thing she didn't want him asking her, the thing she attacked him for trying to do, was suddenly back on the table. He was still interested in her. He was still trying to lasso her in.

For some crazy reason.

"Well, you can ask," she said, pulling back her hair in a nervous fashion.

"And you're cool with it?"

"Wait," Casey said. "Cool with being asked out or cool with actually going on a date?"

"You tell me," he replied.

"I'm lost."

"Come on."

"Normally I'm the one who confuses others," she told him.

"Normally I'm the one who jumps down people's throats," Daniel answered.

She laughed. The more she spoke to him, the more she kinda liked him.

"I promise I'll be . . ."

"What?" Casey asked.

"Less like the me you think I am."

He might have said a hundred other things to make her say no, but he said one thing. One thing that made her actually think about it for a moment.

But it was just for a moment. She wasn't going to forget this summer and the fact that she didn't want to have anything to do with guys. Period.

"I'm sorry," she said. "I just—I don't think that would be a good idea."

Casey had spent enough energy and emotion on the whole Liam thing. The last thing she needed now was to get involved with someone, especially someone like Daniel. Especially during her senior year.

"I should go," Casey said to a silent Daniel.

"Gotta get back to *Melrose Place,* huh?"

"Yes I do," she said, trying not to reveal that there was a smile on her face. "See you around?"

"Okay," Daniel said. "See you around."

Come Together

"YOU EVER GET tired of making all that noise?"

Daniel had stepped out of his room for a moment and suddenly entered a tornado of anger. It was a couple of hours after dinner and his dad was in the eye of the storm. He'd had plenty enough time to come home and drink himself into a frenzy. Another hour or so and he would be sleeping on the warped La-Z-Boy he usually passed out in, the television on and the smell of Daniel's burnt dinner still lingering around. Daniel was used to this routine, of getting a blanket and putting it over his dad while he scooped up the cans of cheap beer on the floor and coffee table.

His father's comment was a loaded one, because Daniel had

been in his room playing his guitar before he'd barked and cursed for him to shut it up.

"It's called practice," Daniel said.

"I got another word for ya—'homework.' Ever hear of that one?"

His two brothers were already out of college and his mom was gone, so they were the only two in the rundown cabin, and Mr. Winter could focus on Daniel alone.

"I didn't have much tonight."

"You say that every night."

Daniel didn't respond as he grabbed a can of pop.

"You're gonna do something with yourself after you graduate," his father barked above the sound of the television. "Just 'cause you pissed away any chance of a football scholarship doesn't mean you're not gonna go to college."

It was ironic Daniel was still being yelled at for getting kicked off the football team—a team he was only on for the sake of his father's pride—because he'd gotten caught drinking on the team bus before a game. There was no way Daniel could have played any kind of college ball unless it involved a Ping-Pong ball and cups of beer.

But hearing his *drunk* father yell at him for following his example—yeah, that was inspiring.

Daniel passed him on the way to his room. There was no talking to him when he was like that. Daniel chose to ignore the things he said, since his dad probably wouldn't remember most of them the next morning.

"You better not fail another class or I'll take that guitar of yours away!"

His father's voice had been loud and clear behind his closed bedroom door. Daniel glanced at the floor and noticed the untouched pre-calculus textbook. Then he had a sinking feeling when he looked at the guitar on his bed.

HIS FATHER'S WARNING continued to echo around in his mind the next day. Daniel sat in the chair with Bobby Tanning sitting in front of him picking his nose—literally just picking it without a care in the world—and thought of the previous night's conversation with his pop.

Daniel felt like he'd been drugged, kidnapped, and dropped into a foreign country every time he sat in Mr. Macklin's pre-calculus class. It wasn't because of the teacher. Mr. Macklin was awesome. His energy and occasional outburst of randomness kept Daniel from falling asleep. Daniel did try. But math had never been his thing, and this wasn't math anymore. This was math on crack.

He'd failed or gotten D's on the last few exams. He hadn't really thought of his grade until his father threatened him. Now he knew he needed to stay after class to talk to the teacher.

Before the class ended, Daniel couldn't help but notice Casey across the room. She was listening to Mr. Macklin and lost in her own thoughts and world and perfect life and perfect grades. Every now and then Daniel thought of their strange run-in at the start of the school year. It was months later, and she was like some pre-calculus equation that Daniel couldn't even begin to figure out.

"YOU ASKED FOR volunteers for Pi Day," Daniel said as Mr. Macklin stood wiping the meticulous notes off the chalkboard.

"I'm glad to see you're excited about math, Daniel."

"Well I, uh, need the extra credit."

"Don't we all," Mr. Macklin said in an optimistic, take-the-bull-by-the-horns sorta way.

Daniel didn't want to have anything to do with bulls. He was like one of those idiots in Spain running like crazy from the bulls in the street.

"What'd you have in mind?"

"I was thinking of writing a song."

Pi Day at TCR had been going on ever since Daniel was a freshman and probably several years before then. He'd had Mr. Macklin his freshman year, and hadn't really paid the math teacher or the March 14 date any attention back then. According to the fun-loving and loud teacher, it was really just an exciting way to get students interested in math. Celebrating the mathematical constant for the ratio of a circle's circumference to its diameter (aka Pi) was kinda corny, but everybody loved Mr. Macklin and his enthusiasm. The highlight of this day would be a celebration in the cafeteria during lunch, where kids would do silly things and eat homemade pies. The year before, a couple of girls did a short play called *The Everlasting Pi*.

As silly as it had seemed, the performance had given Daniel an idea. Since he was bombing pre-calculus, he figured he could score some points writing a song and maybe performing it during lunchtime. Students were already used to Daniel performing every now and then.

"Great idea," Mr. Macklin said. "The students will love it."

"Hopefully."

"I saw your band playing at the Homecoming dance."

"Not really my band, just one I play in."

"Think you'll be able to get it ready in a couple of weeks?"

Daniel thought of his father's threat and wanted to tell the teacher he'd have it done by later that night.

"Yeah, I think so."

Mr. Macklin held up his fist and did something goofy like he always did when the class wasn't paying attention, saying in a serious tone, "Go math."

Before he left, the teacher told Daniel to let him know what he came up with. Daniel had no idea what to write about, but just knew he had to do something. He surely wasn't going to study his way out of failing the class.

A DAY AFTER giving Mr. Macklin a cassette tape of a recording he'd made of the new song, Daniel had been asked to stop by his homeroom at lunchtime. He assumed the teacher had some ideas on it. Daniel knew it wasn't anything great, but he figured it was for extra credit and didn't have to be perfect.

The moment Daniel stepped through the doorway, he stopped, seeing the strawberry blond burst of hair he tried to avoid in the hallways. He felt stupid standing there interrupting them.

"I can come back," he told Mr. Macklin, who was talking with Casey.

"No, no, no—come on in." The teacher stood at his desk and smiled.

Daniel looked at Casey and nodded as he carried his guitar case and put it on the floor next to the teacher's desk. He could feel his face blush, and he never blushed. He never even thought about blushing, but suddenly he was doing both.

"Here's our songwriter," Mr. Macklin said.

"Oh," she said.

That one word—those two little letters—said more than a whole mouthful Casey could have said.

She still thinks I'm a jerk.

"Daniel, I have another interested party who would like to help you with your song."

"No—it's okay," Casey blurted out, her face turning a bit pink. "I'm happy to bake some pies or whatever."

"Don't tell me *you* need extra credit," Daniel said, trying to compose himself and act cool and nonchalant.

Casey looked at him and tightened her lips to smile.

"She wants to keep her GPA up," Mr. Macklin said. "It's fine, I'm sure Daniel won't care if you help out a bit, right?"

Uh, yeah, I do care.

Daniel shrugged as if it was no big deal. He grabbed the guitar he'd found at a thrift store a few years earlier and learned to play by reading a few books. That, and a lot of trial and error. His father would've never gone for lessons. Not for something like music.

"I listened to your song last night and think it's got a nice melody," Mr. Macklin said. "The only thing I'd work on is the lyrics. Casey says she's a poet. So I was thinking she could help you work through some of the lines."

"A poet?" Daniel asked in a mocking tone.

She gave him a forced smile and nodded. "I'm only called in for emergencies."

"I can write another song," Daniel said.

It wasn't like the song was some piece of his heart and soul he'd carved out. It wasn't a song for his band. The music was fine, but Daniel knew the lyrics were a bit—well, lacking.

"No, no, it's good," Mr. Macklin said. "Would you mind playing it for us? So Casey can hear it?"

Casey still sat at her desk, looking like she'd rather be in a prison cell. Daniel nodded, then tried to ignore the fact that Casey was there and would certainly hate the song. But he wasn't there for her. He was doing this for the extra credit.

After he finished the three-minute song, the teacher gave a loud round of applause for him.

"It's great," the always-positive and generous Mr. Macklin said. "It's a catchy little number."

Casey feigned a smile but remained silent.

"I agree—the lyrics are a bit rough," Daniel admitted.

"I love them—they're hilarious. But we probably need to keep them focused on what Pi Day is all about. Casey can help with that."

The song itself had been a catchy little tune he'd written a while ago. The lyrics, however, felt a bit bland and stiff. He'd come up with them in five minutes. It wasn't like he was going to be performing in front of a DJ or a record producer. This was TCR, and half the cafeteria would be zoned out anyway.

"Daniel, what do you think of working with our poet laureate here on some of those lyrics? Would you mind?"

Yeah, I'd mind because, see, this girl here hates me and I've been avoiding her ever since the start of school.

"Sure," Daniel said.

"I don't need to work on the song if he's happy with it," Casey said.

"She just doesn't want to hang out with me," Daniel couldn't help adding.

"I never said that."

Daniel kept looking at Mr. Macklin, who had an amused look on his face. "Her boyfriend might not like us singing together."

"I think we're supposed to write a song about Pi Day, right?" Casey quickly said, her feisty cap back on. "And I don't believe I have a boyfriend."

Daniel knew Casey had been talking to Liam. Yes, he avoided her, but he still paid attention to her.

"Why don't you two figure out a time to work on the song?" Mr. Macklin said. "Then surprise me on the day by performing it."

"I don't sing," Casey said.

"You have to sing if you want extra credit," Daniel said.

She glared at him.

"You'll do great," Mr. Macklin said. "Come on—they'll love it."

Daniel held his guitar and suddenly found this amusing.

There was no way Casey was going to be able to do this. He was going to make sure of it. Little Miss Sunshine wasn't going to get her extra credit, because she would get sick and tired of the guy she would have to be performing with.

"Can't wait," Daniel said with a face full of phony glee.

"SO WHAT ARE we supposed to do now?"

Daniel sat in the empty music room facing Casey. She'd been late, of course, and for a few moments he'd thought about bailing on her. She finally showed up out of breath with some story about a friend who needed something or other. It was just girl talk. Suddenly she didn't even know why she was there.

"You're supposed to help me write this song," Daniel said.

"Don't be smug. I know that. But how?"

"You tell me. This was your idea."

"This was Mr. Macklin's idea. Before I knew you were writing the song."

"Oh, well, I'm so sorry it was me," Daniel said.

"I didn't mean it like that," Casey said. "I just—I know you've been avoiding me like the plague."

"Uh, wait a minute—I'm not the one who acted like I have the plague."

She brushed back her hair and gave him an animated grin as she stood behind a chair. "Can we just work on the song?" she asked.

She was still the same Casey. Cute and charming and a bit like cotton candy. Sweet until you had too much of it. Sweet until you had a stomachache.

Casey sat down and took out a notebook from her backpack.

"Don't tell me you've got a bunch of song lyrics you're expecting me to try and do something with," Daniel said.

"Well, I can't write music. Plus, the music is fine."

"'Fine'?"

She rolled her eyes. "It was beautiful, the most amazing song I've *ever* heard."

"Shut up."

"You admitted the lyrics needed some work."

"Oh, this is gonna be good."

"Maybe you'll be pleasantly surprised," Casey said, moving over and taking a seat next to Daniel. "English is my favorite subject."

"Do you know anything about math?"

"I know enough," Casey said. "Plus—the point isn't to educate. The point is to get positive interest. To intrigue the rest of the students."

"Mr. Macklin say that?"

The cute, freckle-faced girl just shook her head and rolled her eyes. "Of course not. But people will start throwing food if we start talking about the one million digits of Pi."

"Do you know how to play the guitar?" he asked.

"Nope. But who knows. Maybe one day I'll learn. Maybe you could even teach me."

"You can't afford my fees."

"So play me your song again."

Part of Daniel still thought this was some kind of practical joke. He took his guitar and played her the song again. At the end, she gave him a nod and started writing in her journal.

"Not bad," Casey said.

He wasn't sure to tell her *thanks* or *why don't you try it?* Before he could say anything, Casey started talking.

"The song is fun and sticks in your head. The lyrics are dreadful."

"Please, tell me what you really think," Daniel said.

"'It's Pi Day and I gotta say. It's time to bring in the hay.' What does that even mean, 'bring in the hay'?"

He shrugged. "It rhymes."

She made a gagging sound. "We can come up with something better than *that*."

"Thanks a lot."

"Come on, Daniel. Were you even trying to be serious?"

"You know how Mr. Macklin always makes up lyrics to songs in class. He was just doing this the other day to Coolio."

"'Time to bring in the hay.' A second-grader would ask what that means."

"Okay—then you give it a try."

"'There's something in the way that silly number sounds today.'" She paused and wrote it down." That's not bad. Not very good, but not bad."

Daniel didn't say anything. He had been positive that Casey Sparkland was out of his life for good. Apparently, for some reason, she wasn't.

And deep down, if he really had to admit it, he was quite all right with that.

THEY'D BEEN WORKING on lyrics for about half an hour, or more like Daniel had been listening to Casey suggest better lyrics, when he decided to stop things and ask a question.

"So tell me. What kind of music do you like?"

"Total country," Casey said. Then she pointed at the boots she was wearing with her long dress. "Can't you tell?"

"I wasn't sure if you were wearing those boots because of a dare or what. It's better not to say anything when it comes to the outfits."

"Stop it." Casey could tell he was teasing and rolled her eyes like she did every few minutes.

"I can't stand country," Daniel said.

"You have no taste, then."

"Oh, come on. See—that's the problem. You're trying to make this into some country ballad."

"That's better than the song you had. I don't think we could find a category for that one."

"So you only listen to country?"

"No, not only."

They discussed music for a while, then began arguing over the quality of certain artists. While he was trying to make a point to Casey about rock music, she stopped him.

"I have to go soon."

"Have a date?" Daniel asked.

"Funny. But I usually don't go out on dates on Wednesday nights."

"I don't know—I mean, those country girls like to honky-tonk and line dance."

She looked like she was smelling something sour. "What are you talking about?"

"Okay, fine. Let's finish this line. The last thing was the complex line."

"'So complex and intricate.'"

Daniel played the chorus again, humming to it. "So complex and intricate, you're too legit to quit."

"I love it!"

Daniel looked up. "Really?"

"No."

He played it again.

"How about "'So complex and intricate, an infinite number going on.'"

"So technical."

"It works, right?" Casey asked. "'So complex and intricate, an infinite number going on. We celebrate the mystery that's you, by writing you this Pi song.'"

"'They mystery that's you'? I don't know."

"Oh, that's great," Casey said.

"Do I get a say here?"

"Not really."

He played it with those lyrics, but Casey stood up and shook her head, waving her hand.

"Play it again, but give it a little life."

"Excuse me? Life?" He sped up the song and made it sound entirely different, like a song out of a Chipmunks episode.

"Okay, now you're just being obnoxious. Give it some energy. Give it something—I don't know. Anything more than the brooding thing it's got going on."

"Don't country singers do the brooding thing?"

Casey flipped her hair back, something he estimated she did four hundred times an hour. "Maybe romantic brooding, not death-march brooding."

He took his guitar and offered it to her. "Look, why don't you try it?"

"I'm just trying to help," she said. "I'm just trying to make it the best song possible."

"Yes. Obviously. I mean—gotta make sure you get that A." He wasn't sure if she was starting to drive him crazy or simply making him like her more.

"You don't have to give me so much attitude."

"You made it clear you didn't want to have anything to do with me last time we spoke."

"No, I didn't. Since when?"

"Since you said you'd see me around and then waited until we got stuck writing a song together."

Casey sighed and crossed her arms. For a moment she glanced at the door with its sliver of a glass window in it. "I had just broken up with Liam and wasn't really wanting to do that whole thing again."

"I heard you two were back together again."

"You heard wrong."

He thought of mentioning seeing them together at a party a month ago, but he didn't. Or about the times he had seen them talking by her locker. But no. Daniel shook his head and glanced at her. "Okay—well, here—what if I take that last bit of the song—the twenty-second thing you actually approve of—and keep going with it."

"Play that part again. Make it longer."

"You like giving orders, don't you?" he asked.

"When it's the right order to give, sure."

Daniel couldn't help but laugh.

He played the simple chords over and over again. She wrote in her notebook, stared out at the chalkboard in front of them, then wrote a little more.

"That's great. I can come up with something tonight for it." She scribbled something else down.

"What do you mean, 'something tonight'? Are you going to share?"

"Yes, tomorrow. Same place and same time."

"You'll be late," Daniel said, excited she wanted to meet again tomorrow night.

"You'll be waiting," Casey said as she got ready to leave.

Yes, I will.

CASEY HAD TRIED to get out of singing, but in the end, the two of them would go on to perform the song simply called "The Pi Song" to an excited audience in the cafeteria. Mr. Macklin stood by the wall, giving his piercing whistle and raising his hands in a cheer. Casey had a soft and subtle voice, but she could sing.

In the middle of the song, Daniel looked over at her and caught her gaze.

For a moment, they weren't in the cafeteria around five hundred or so students.

For a moment, she wasn't this girl who had kept avoiding him and making it clear she didn't want to have anything to do with him.

He played the guitar and sang into one of the microphones Mr. Macklin had set up for them and he smiled at Casey.

You're doing great, his smile said.

He could tell she was nervous so he simply nodded and kept guiding her along.

When they finished and heard the applause, it was a pretty cool thing. Especially for a silly little song like the one they had written.

But they wrote it. *They.* Casey and Daniel.

The students loved it and Mr. Macklin whooped and hollered after the performance, giving both of them giant hugs.

After the lunch period, Daniel told her thanks as they began walking toward their next classes.

"That actually turned out pretty good," he said.

"Call me anytime you need some more lyrics."

"So you want to be my Bernie Taupin?"

"Your what?" Casey asked.

"Oh, come on. Do I have to keep educating you on music? You've heard of Elton John, right?"

"I told you I'm a country girl."

"Maybe that's why you turned me down," he said. "You're afraid of boys who like a little rock and roll."

"I'm not afraid of any boys, Mr. Winter." She gave him that testy, humoring look.

For just a split second, Daniel thought of asking her out again. But she walked down the hallway away from him before he could say anything else. Just like before, Casey Sparkland was there one moment and gone the next.

Got a Hold on Me

FOR A MONTH, from Pi Day to spring break, Casey had been able to forget about guys. But five minutes after stepping foot back at school, a face from the past grinned and said good morning.

"Have a nice break?" a tall and tanned Liam asked her.

"Probably not as nice as your trip to Mexico."

"I was thinking about you the whole time."

Casey let out a fake laugh, but she knew she was nervous. Things between them had been friendly the last few months. Violet had dumped him around Christmas, and it had taken her a couple of months to finally give in and start talking to the guy. But his comment surprised her.

"Look, I was thinking—I've been doing a lot of thinking," Liam said. "Would you go to prom with me?"

She wanted to shake her head and say no. She wanted to tell this guy he should have thought about that before he decided to trade her for someone like Violet. She wanted to gasp and let out a shocking laugh and then keep laughing and laughing until he was gone.

"Okay."

The word escaped her mouth before she had time to process it.

Okay? Okay, as in yes? As in, you're okay for being such a loser but okay, let's go to prom?

"That's awesome. We're gonna have a blast."

Liam's handsome mug gave her a charming smile and she couldn't help loving it.

What am I doing?

"I'll swing by later after first period. Okay?"

Liam went strolling away while Casey stood there, speechless, glancing into her open locker, wondering why she hadn't already closed the door.

IT WAS PAST midnight a couple of nights later and Casey still couldn't sleep. She felt like she'd just had one of those massive chocolate coffee drinks from Starbucks and was too wired to go to bed. She didn't need caffeine keeping her awake. The worry was doing a great job of that.

She hadn't intended to go to the prom this year, even if it was her senior year. She would have been fine sitting it out, or going by herself. Everything in her had said there was absolutely no way she would end up going with him. But when Liam had asked, she had said yes without even having to think about it.

So Casey couldn't blame anybody but herself for this mess she'd gotten herself into.

A part of her knew Liam would always come back around. Once Violet got bored with Liam and his controlling ways, he would start calling and trying to cross paths with her again. The thing that surprised her was that she let him. The thing that stunned her was that she actually said yes when he asked her to prom.

But then when Daniel and his sweet and funny face came out of nowhere earlier that day and asked her . . .

Is there a way I can go with two guys?

It had happened at the end of the day. Daniel showed up by her locker out of the blue. She knew something was up because Daniel never just casually walked by her. She'd put an end to that on the first day of school.

"Hey, I was wondering if you had plans for prom."

The question had made her want to do one of two things: either laugh out loud at the irony of this question, or sprint down the hallway and avoid answering altogether.

Instead, she'd answered with a "Not exactly."

Casey stared up into the darkness of her room and wondered what "Not exactly" actually meant.

I'm an idiot.

"Well, if you don't—I'd love to take you to prom. If you're interested."

She thought of the look that had probably been on her face. Casey knew her face had been flushed, that was obvious. There was also probably a look of surprise and amusement and confusion all mixed up into a stammering, blushing response of "Well, let me—yeah—just—yeah I'm not sure at this—right now."

Poor Daniel. The guy always seemed to follow in Liam's unfortunate wake. Daniel had waited for an interpretation of her response, but none came.

"Okay," he eventually said, not exactly sure what kind of answer she'd given him. "I guess you can just let me know."

"Yeah, I'd love to go."

Those words had been like a bird in a cage suddenly being let free. They flew out and suddenly were gone.

Casey knew she would have to call Daniel soon and let him know the truth.

I can't call the poor guy again only to say no to him. Again.

Yet a part of her knew she couldn't cancel her plans with Liam. There was a chance—just a slight chance—that things were going to be okay with him. He had made some mistakes and behaved like an idiot and he was sorry. He had apologized repeatedly and promised Casey it would never happen again.

There was a possible future with Liam. Daniel was just a cute guy she barely knew. Sure, there were some sparks during their songwriting sessions. That had been fun and silly and it had provided some levity in a boring school year. That was it, however. There wasn't anything more that would ever happen with her and Daniel.

My parents know and love Liam. I've never once mentioned Daniel to Mom and Dad.

She tried to figure out a way to tell Daniel. She wanted to call him and get it over with, yet Casey knew the best thing to do was to talk with him in person. He deserved that much. She would try to tell him how confused she was with the whole prom thing, and how Liam and her were just starting to work things out.

Daniel will understand.

She kept telling herself this. But somehow, Casey was the one who didn't seem to understand.

AS IT TURNED out, Daniel didn't understand the prom thing either.

Casey had decided to talk with him around lunchtime the following day, expecting to get a simple and polite "okay" out of him. She explained that she had been asked to go to prom a couple days earlier by Liam, then shared how she had said yes even though she wasn't sure she was going to go.

"So you're actually going with him?" Daniel said in surprise.

It wasn't just a casual surprise. The way Daniel looked and sounded, he appeared stunned.

"We're working things out."

"Didn't you tell me you couldn't even stand looking at him?"

"Did I say that?"

Daniel nodded, his narrow eyes more expressive than usual. "Yeah. That and a lot of other things."

"I talk a lot."

"What exactly are you guys working out?"

"Just stuff. It's complicated."

Daniel laughed, then looked around. He thought for a few moments as he nodded.

"What?" Casey asked.

"It's not that complicated. The guy dumped you for a sophomore who's been with half the guys at this school."

"How would you know that?"

"How would—are you insinuating anything?"

"I don't have to *insinuate* a thing. I'm saying it outright."

"Sorry. The only girls I go for are the fiery ones who can't stand me. You know—the ones who laugh in my face the first time I walk up to them. Those are my dream girls. I just can't seem to get enough of them."

"Oh really?" Casey was angry now, and she couldn't care less how loud they were being or who was watching.

"Yeah, the problem is there aren't too many of those kinds of girls around here. Girls like Violet are a dime a dozen. But those temperamental, moody, redheaded ones—no, those are hard to find."

"I'm not *redheaded*. I happen to be strawberry blond, thank you very much."

"Glad you recognize yourself," Daniel said.

She'd never noticed how tall he was, or exactly how handsome he looked. Standing there in his cut-up jeans and UNC Tarheels T-shirt, Casey thought Daniel looked adorable. The scowl on his face, the anger in his eyes, and the determination to stay and talk this out.

She hated him in a strange, loving way.

"You really know how to make a girl feel great about herself."

"What?" Daniel laughed even louder this time. "A girl who gets treated like that by some smug jerk needs to be in therapy. Hey—have fun at the prom. You two deserve each other."

This time Daniel didn't wait for a response. He walked away before he could hear her come back with another insult.

Casey stood there for a few moments, wondering how this had happened. Wondering if the things Daniel had said were true. Wondering why she kept wondering about this guy named Daniel Winter.

My sweet soul-filled getaway
You're my answer to tomorrow
My sun-filled holiday
—Sparkland & Winter, "My Holiday"

PRESENT DAY

Daniel the Dreamer

IT TAKES THREE messages and a few more e-mails in the course of a couple of days to finally hear back from Gary, my manager.

"Hey buddy, what's going on?"

There are so many things wrong with this opening line from Gary that I almost tell him *exactly* what's wrong.

You've been ignoring me for months and it takes half a dozen tries to get your attention and now you're calling me buddy with the smooth Southern sweet-talk, casually wondering what's wrong.

The problem is that beggars can't be choosers, and I'm one big fat beggar.

"Thanks for calling me back," I tell him.

"Yeah, sure, no problem. I'm out in California. Only got your messages now."

Uh-huh. And I have a plot of land in the Antarctic I'd like you to buy.

"I hate to bother you 'cause I know you're so busy."

"Oh it's fine," he lies. "What's up?"

I wonder why I really have to ask. He knows why I'm calling, because I've stated it pretty clearly in my e-mails and voice mails. So I repeat what I've been asking.

"Have you had a chance to listen to my demos?"

Pause the conversation and this whole scene. This question could be the question asked by any musician anywhere over and over again. The thing is this. Gary has specifically asked me over the years for demos. He wants more songs from me. At least, he used to, especially after he was able to sell the first couple.

"Yeah, yeah I did." He sounds like he's walking across a busy freeway out there in California. "There were some decent songs. Not bad. Not bad at all."

"But not particularly good?"

"Here's the thing, buddy. Nothing stood out. Nothing screamed at me. They all felt too—I don't know . . ."

"Boring?"

"No, man, they were fine songs. But they were . . . safe. Easy. To nail a song these days isn't easy. You have songwriters cranking seven days a week trying to nail them."

"I'm going to have more time to work on them." I regret this statement the moment I say it.

Gary doesn't care about how much time I do or don't have. He cares about how much time he has, and right now I'm wasting it.

"Look, I can polish some of those off and try to rework them."

There's a pause that feels like an agonizing year. For someone who talks fast and moves fast and thinks fast, a pause is a very bad thing.

"Daniel, I love you, buddy, I really do."

Oh, please, not the "I love you, man" shtick.

"We need something as witty and fun as 'My Holiday,'" he tells me.

"I think you told me that last time we spoke. And the time before that."

"It's true. I'm sorry, but that's the truth. That's what happens when you write a song that becomes a big hit."

And the truth is that song didn't just happen to come to me.

It came to us. Meaning Winter and Sparkland.

"What's your little writing partner up to?"

"I don't know," I tell him.

"Maybe you should know."

Maybe you should stay out of my personal business.

"I doubt she's going to want to write another song anytime soon."

"Man, that sucks, bro 'cause you two have something special."

"Something that's missing in my songs?"

He sounds out of breath and a bit annoyed. "Just being honest, buddy."

"I can give you a Sparkland/Winter song."

"Okay."

"No, I'm serious," I tell him.

"All right, man. Then do it. You play me something special. Give me something to work with."

"I'm driving to my father's. What if I stopped by?"

"If you have a good enough song to play me, then stop by anytime." He laughs as if he's joking. "I'm giving you a hard time, you know that."

"A week. I'll have something to you. I promise."

"Can't wait, buddy. Just tell me something."

"Yeah."

"How are you feeling? Honestly?"

Gary's question seems a bit odd and out of the blue.

"Why?"

"You feeling happy? Or sad?"

"I'm not sure."

I'm lying because I totally know exactly how I feel but I'd rather not admit that.

"Put the emotion in the song," Gary says. "The more emotion the better. Adele broke up with her boyfriend and immediately went into the studio. Wrote 'Someone Like You.'"

I chuckle for a moment, remembering *Saturday Night Live*'s spoof of that song. That's how much it's seeped into pop culture.

"Yeah, no pressure there," I say.

"I got pressure on me twenty-four seven, but that's the business, buddy."

After I tell him good-bye, I stare at my cell phone and decide I officially hate the term "buddy."

It dawns on me this is probably my final shot with my "buddy" and "bro" Gary Mains. Now all I have to do is write a song worthy of being bought and sold by a big-name musician.

No problem, right?

A FEW DAYS after being fired from *Dandee Donuts* and the night before I leave to go back home to Asheville to be with my father, my closest friend in Seattle offers encouragement in his own typical way.

"The problem is you're a dreamer."

I met Harvey Johnson a year ago at a Sting concert a group of us from work attended. He was one of the few guys I'd met in the city who wasn't married and didn't have kids. It's not like I have anything against either of those kinds of people, but sometimes there's not much to add to the conversation when it's all about baby food and car seats and preschool.

For a second I glance at him sprawled out on my couch and notice he doesn't realize he just insulted me. "Maybe the world needs more dreamers."

He curses and sips his beer. "You kiddin' me? Everybody's a dreamer. Because everybody is just one shot away from being the next American Idol. The next Top Model. The next *big thing*. A Twitter sensation. A YouTube phenom. Everybody dreams. Everybody."

"What about you?"

"Nope."

"No dreams at all?"

"Not at all."

"That's kinda sad."

For a moment, he looks at me, then he stares at my suitcases and boxes waiting by the front door of my apartment. I have to laugh.

"Yeah, I know, I'm not exactly the picture of success."

"Dreams come with baggage, my friend. I just don't want to be stuck with a bunch of suitcases when all the doors shut."

I drink my beer and think this might be the best thing Harvey's ever thought of. "So if I come back to Seattle, can I find a place to crash?"

"Of course. Rent-free. Unless I'm married."

"You have to date first before that happens."

"Not necessarily. I'll find a mail-order bride from Russia."

I laugh and change the playlist on my iPod. Tom Petty begins playing.

"I just need to write one great song," I say. "A song like this one."

"You've written a bunch of great songs."

I shake my head. "I've cowritten some beauties. But not like this one."

"Runnin' Down a Dream" seems to put an exclamation point on what I'm saying.

"So what's stopping you then?" Harvey says, his curly explosion of hair sticking out from the chair he's sitting in.

"I'm heading back home to take care of my dying pop. I'm

going to be a nurse for who-knows-how-long. That doesn't inspire a lot of love for songwriting."

"So take some detours before you get home. Go get inspired."

"Inspiration doesn't help. I've been inspired all my life. Look where it's taken me."

Harvey curses in disbelief. "I say the great song is out there. Go find it. Go write it. Make it your own. Don't think you need someone to help you write it."

"I've been trying for thirty-five years, man."

"So you got a little more time left before you start serving Arby's sauce to customers."

I laugh. He's using my line. "Maybe that's what I should be writing about. An epic love song dedicated to curly fries."

"That would be a number-one hit."

There's some truth in our joke, as painful as it might sound.

THE DOOR TO the deck is open and I hear the gentle sound of drizzle. Harvey is sleeping off his beers but I can't sleep. I find myself thinking of Casey, of Seattle, of the map of my life. I wish there were a rulebook for living, a dummy's guide for growing up and getting a clue. All I'd acquired over the years was a messy collection of memories cowritten with my inspiration and muse.

I'd call her if I had her number, but she changed that long ago when she wanted to get as far away from me as possible. I remember that final text I sent her back at the country music festival I got us tickets for. It seems like that was two centuries ago, not just two years. I have no idea where Casey is or what she's doing. Which is probably for the best.

I go back inside and scan my bedroom to make sure I have everything. The big pieces of furniture I'm leaving behind. I asked my landlord if that was okay. Last thing I want to do is haul an old couch or bed across the country for no reason. I see an assortment of old photos I found in a drawer lying next to my wallet on the dresser. For a second, I stare at the picture of Casey.

I think I miss her smile most of all. The smile directed at me. The one that says she's proud of me. Another that says she can't believe she's laughing at what I said or did, that she can't believe I made her laugh again. Another that says I'm full of it and I know it. Another that says she loves me and always will.

I sit on the edge of my bed, knowing there's no way I can ever stop thinking of her. Love is like that favorite song you know by heart and can hum in your sleep. The lyrics change and the chords move, but the tune always sounds the same.

I write out a few lyrics to a could-be song on my iPhone.

I might no longer be employed, but I don't need a paycheck to make music.

Go find it. Go write it. Make it your own.

Yet the same voice comes back.

I just need Casey.

My partner and collaborator and friend and love. Filling out the loose ends and brightening up the picture and smoothing out the rough edges and connecting the dots of my broken soul.

My creative crutch.

I'm restless and not tired, so I head back out on my deck to feel the rain on my face. The night seems to sigh, as if it knows how silly and stupid I'm being. I know God knows too, but I've been keeping Him an arm's length away, afraid of having to give my heart and soul over to someone completely.

Maybe in that way, Casey and I are just alike.

A Changed Casey

ONE MINUTE, YOU can be choking with anger and flushed with furious tears, screaming at the man you gave your life to, telling him you never want to see him again. Then, time can blink and you can find yourself sitting at the end of a dining room table right next to this same man, talking about how teaching is going and how your family is doing and all the wonderful little sweet stories there are to talk about in your life. This is life, and it doesn't always make sense, and even when it does, it can seem complex and confusing.

I've been talking more than Burke, but that's because he's been asking questions. He knows I can't help myself, especially when I'm nervous. I'll ramble on and on until there's nothing left to say or do. I think I'm trying to do that now even though we've already finished our plates full of the variety of warmed-up leftovers we had.

"I need to just stop talking," I say.

"I like hearing you talk."

I laugh. "You once said I never let you get in a word."

"Casey—"

"And you were probably right."

Burke has these dark eyes that can be bewitching one moment and menacing the next. He's a deliberate person, even when he's drinking. The way he sits across from me, the way he stares and uses silence to his advantage. The way he's acting like he's a changed man.

"There's a lot that's happened to me over these past four years," Burke says.

"Four years is a long time." I say this even though my four years have seemed like the same song sung over a thousand times.

"I started going to church again."

I nod and raise my eyebrows. "Glad to hear it."

"It's been almost nine months now. Ever since I found out about Dad's cancer."

We tried going to church, and we tried to go to counseling. Burke didn't want to have a part of either of those things. His life was too busy and he was too preoccupied to worry too much about how any of that stuff related to us. Until, of course, it was way too late.

"I'm not asking you to move in with me tonight," he says.

"Good thing, because that's not happening. Even this meal—I need to leave pretty soon."

"You once told me you weren't ever going to give up on me."

"I haven't. That's why I'm here. But giving up on you is a whole other thing than giving up on *us*. You and I are a whole other subject. An entirely different story."

"Can there be a sequel?"

"No. That story was told. It ended in a tragedy."

"We're still here. We're still being civil. We're still—I don't know—I can feel there's a chemistry."

Burke is right, of course. There's always been that chemistry, since the first day I spoke with him on campus at Duke. He was the freshman quarterback everybody was talking about. I assumed he'd completely forget about me as soon as he stopped talking to me. I was still dating Daniel and I wasn't interested. But there had been something, and that *something* was the thing that kept Burke and me on each other's radar. He kept pursuing me, and I loved that pursuit, to be honest.

There comes a point in your life, however, when you no longer want to be chased after. You're too tired from running. You need to stop and stay put and feel the security around you.

"I'm always going to love you, Burke. In some way. But I just—I can't. I can't go down that road again. I didn't expect any of this to even come up. I thought you'd be here and I would see you and get this will taken care of, and I'd be gone."

"Stay with me tonight."

I laugh and roll my eyes. "You're still the same."

"So are you."

It's been years since he's given me that look. That look of wanting me and needing me. A part of me feels hooked, like he's got me on the line and is slowly and surely reeling me in.

"I'm not the same person who you tossed to the curb," I tell him.

This makes him look down for a moment, then take another drink. "That's a harsh way of putting it."

"It was pretty harsh to have to live through."

"I'm sorry."

"Yeah, I know. A lot has happened. I enjoy my life now. I enjoy where I'm living. I enjoy where I'm teaching."

"But you're all alone?"

"I'm still close to my parents and my sisters. If you're asking whether I have someone to wait up for or clean up after or worry whether they're seeing someone else, then my answer is yes, I'm on my own."

He curses and laughs. "Woo-eee. You're still like taking a shot of some strong drink. You still got a bite."

"Thank you for dinner."

"Thank all the relatives and friends who came over."

I want to ask him if he's truly all alone, like he asked me. I want to ask him about his health, things like his drinking habits and his insomnia and the nightmares he had when we were together. But questions like that feel too intimate, and intimacy with Burke is a dangerous thing because it can lead to more intimacy. Even though there is a chemistry there, as he had said, there can be more no more intimacy with this man. Not after everything that happened.

We eventually take our plates to the kitchen and I help him clean up. I keep my distance and make sure it's not one of these romantic cleaning-up-the-kitchen bits of foreplay that always plays out in film. This is just washing the dishes. Then I'll be leaving.

Before I can say good-bye, Burke takes my hand.

"Just listen—please, Casey, listen to me, okay?"

I don't want to look him in the eyes, but I'm forced to because I just can't help myself. I've spent enough time away from him, trying to forget about those eyes, but right here and now they're right in front of me like piercing headlights. I look at him and brace for the impact of his words.

"I can change and I have been starting to change, but yes—I got a long ways to go. So do you and I. *We* can change. We can still have that future we were talking about once. A family. A future."

"Burke—"

"I mean it. I'm ready. I'm not asking for everything this very minute or tomorrow. I'm just asking that you give me a little time. That you don't immediately shut the door. That you give me a chance."

"You never gave me a chance," I remind him.

"I know. But isn't that what you call grace?"

He's using our past and my faith to his advantage. Yet I can't say he's not making a point.

"I didn't want my father to die, and I never expected him to leave both of us this place. I'm not asking because I want this house. I just—couldn't you see living here? The two of us? You wouldn't have to work—if you didn't want to—you could work on your writing. This would be a pretty peaceful place to work."

After all this time, he's suddenly talking about my writing.

Burke keeps going, perhaps seeing the resistance on my face.

"I know you're staying in Hilton Head for a few days and all I ask is that you let me come back into your life," Burke says. "Don't slam the door shut like I did. Let's just—just think about it. Okay? Just try and think about it."

"Burke, this house—"

"Just think about it. All of it. Okay. Don't make any decisions now."

There are so many things I want to say, but all I do is nod and clench my car keys and then stand up to leave.

Guess you were a star
Waiting to fall into my arms
The sand under my feet
A beachside-bought charm
—Sparkland & Winter, "My Holiday"

High School

and the Rooftop

(1996)

Fool That I Am

IT WAS ELEVEN o'clock at night when Casey walked into the house, trying to be quiet. Her heels tapped on the wood floor, so she took them off and suddenly became three inches shorter. The long red prom dress sashayed even when she didn't want to have anything to do with sashing or swaying. Casey walked into the family room and sat down on the couch for a moment, letting out a sigh and rubbing her tired feet.

"Case."

The whisper startled her. She turned around and saw her mom wearing a robe and squinting at the light in the room.

"Did I wake you?" Casey asked, standing up.

"I wasn't really sleeping." Her mom looked at the grandfather clock. "You're home early."

"Yeah."

"How'd it go?"

"I'm just glad it's over."

Casey walked back to pick up her shoes. She always told her mom everything and planned to tell her everything in the morning. It was still nighttime, however, and Casey wanted to be left alone.

"I'm sorry to hear that."

For a second, Casey shook her head and stared up at the ceiling. "I should've known better. It was my own fault."

"Did something happen?"

Telling her mom wouldn't have been a five-minute story. It would probably be an hour-long conversation full of tears and anger. Then it would probably morph into a conversation—another conversation—about her parents. Then there would be more tears and more anger and . . .

"Can I talk about it in the morning?" Casey asked. "I'm tired."

"Of course."

Casey couldn't wait to unpeel her dress and finally be free again. She wanted to leave the dress and this night and Liam all behind.

"Casey—things like prom—they never live up to the hype."

For a moment, Casey just looked at her. Her mother was still very pretty, despite the wrinkles of worry and regret wrapped around her eyes. The last year had obviously taken a toll on her physically. She looked a bit too thin, her skin a bit too pale.

"I think that's just sad," Casey said. "Some things should be better than the hype."

"I know," her mother said, putting her arm around her. "But sometimes people let you down."

"I know. And I hate knowing that. I hate having to rely on others."

"Rely on God and He'll give you peace."

Casey stopped and looked at her. "Do you have it?"

Casey's mother gave her a tired smile, then a slow nod. "Every little bit I have is from Heaven above. I'll take what I can get."

THE FIRST TIME Casey slipped outside her bedroom window and scrambled onto the roof was three years ago, after hearing a rather nasty argument between her parents. Her window opened up right above the covering to the front porch. Since the slope wasn't too steep, she could safely crawl out onto the shingles and then climb a bit to make it to the top of their garage, which overlooked the front and side of the house. Her parents didn't like her going out there, but that hadn't stopped her from doing it.

Lately, Casey had been slipping out the window often, looking up at a sky full of stars and asking God for some answers. Asking God for some peace. But God didn't seem to be interested in giving her any. At least, not anytime soon.

After changing into some loose sweatpants and a T-shirt, Casey felt like her old self again, not some made-up Barbie trying to fit in and be someone she would never be. She wondered if she had ever been herself around Liam, or if she had tried living up to this idea of what it meant to be his girlfriend. He was popular and good-looking and funny, but she wasn't sure why she had ever fallen for someone so smug and so insensitive.

She sat in her regular spot, on the side of the house where she could see the stars lighting up their yard. The trees towered and made a fence on each side of their lawn. A huge oak sat on the opposite side of their house. Her father had threatened to cut it down when they moved in, but her mother wouldn't let him. Each year they needed to trim a little off it, since it was so close to the house.

Casey often wondered what it would be like to pack her things and slip down that tree and off into the night. Not that she really wanted to run away from her family or her life. She would be going to Duke in the fall, and she would finally be free.

But Liam's going too, and wasn't that always the plan?

She didn't want to think of plans at the moment. She didn't want to think of school, of making sure she got good grades, of making sure everybody liked her, of taking very good care to be everything she could be.

So who am I? Really?

The after-prom party she had left was surely still raging, and all her friends were there, probably laughing and talking and having a great time. Yet Casey sat on her roof wondering how she could have spent so much time on a boy who was such a waste of talent and potential.

You're just angry. You'll get over it tomorrow.

School was almost over, however. She wasn't going back to Liam. Enough was enough. She would graduate and would go to college and would end up finding a whole other life.

She just wished she felt good about that. Casey wanted to have just a little peace. Just a few more answers.

There was no way she could ever end up like her parents. No way.

If there was one thing she wanted to work in her life, it was that.

Even if *that* no longer included the boy she always thought it would.

I'm on Fire

DANIEL DROVE HIS car around like some kind of fool, fiddling with the radio, looking for the right station to land on, but having no luck. He didn't mind skipping prom that night, since there was nobody he wanted to go with. Yet he still felt restless, like there was something he should be doing or somewhere he should be going. The last thing he wanted to do was be stuck at home with his cranky father yelling at him to turn down the music. In his beat-up Camaro, Daniel could crank the music up and try to keep out the unease about life after high school.

There was really nothing to be worried about. For the time being, he would be going to a local junior college, and he was planning on getting a job to make some money. He'd also start getting serious about the band and doing something with it. Rex would be attending the same junior college as Daniel. Rex had no real ambitions or goals or plans. He could play the drums, but he didn't want to do it his whole life. Daniel needed to find a musician who he connected with and could write songs with.

Write songs with . . .

Once he thought it, he hated himself for thinking about her. Somehow Casey had cast some voodoo spell on his head and he hadn't been able to get rid of it. She popped up in his mind all the time, and when she didn't, she suddenly seemed to pass him by at school. He pictured her slow-dancing with Liam and laughing with their little clique. One last farewell dance. One last kiss. One last "I love you." It all made him want to throw up.

Thank God I'm not there.

So she made him laugh. So she made the temperature in the room suddenly rise. So she was impossible *not* to like. Yeah, he hated Casey Sparkland, but only because she annoyed him. She annoyed him for not paying him more attention and not having any interest in him whatsoever. She irritated him because even though everybody seemed to know what a complete loser Liam was, Casey obviously still was madly in love with the guy.

Good riddance.

He tried to say this and believe he meant it. Yet even as he did, he found himself driving closer to her neighborhood, then driving down her street. He knew where she lived. He had passed by her house before. The driveway sloped down from this semi-private drive in the woods. This neighborhood and her large house made it clear why Casey didn't fit into his life.

Daniel knew it was pretty stupid to be doing this. Surely she knew his car, and surely he'd be recognized if she was home.

They're out having fun and being teenagers and finding love all over again.

That was a lyric. Maybe. He wished he had something to write down the thought, but he didn't. He'd forget it like all the other potential lyrics that came through his mind and then evaporated. He'd move on and forget it ever happened. Just like this past year. Just like T. C. Roberson.

He didn't turn off the lights on his car as he drove past Casey's house. He knew this was a bit creepy, like some stalker checking to see if she was home. Daniel knew he wasn't a stalker, however. He was just curious. And maybe a bit hopeful.

And how about a whole lot of stupid.

There was no car in the driveway. He couldn't help looking at the front door and then looking at the silent windows, closed like sleeping eyes. Then he noticed something white on the roof right above the three-car garage.

He cursed and drove into the curb as he noticed it was Casey sitting there on the roof. Sitting there watching him drive by, watching him slow the car down and look out and be stalker boy.

Grabbing the steering wheel, he wanted to peel out off down the road.

Get back on the road first, you fool.

He corrected the car but kept looking up.

Then the worst thing happened.

She waved.

I'm a total loser, and from here on out she's gonna think I'm just a complete knob.

Daniel waved back, as if he was cool and this was normal and waving at a girl on the roof after midnight was the sort of thing that happened to him on a daily basis.

With the house and Casey passing him by, Daniel thought about things. Then he figured *why not*. He stopped the car on the edge of the driveway. He climbed out of the car and walked down the circling drive toward her.

Hopefully she would still be there sitting on the roof. And then—well, who knows what would happen then. Maybe he could at least say hi in person.

You Don't Even Know
Who I Am

*H*E HAD WALKED up to the side of the house she was sitting on and greeted her as if it was any ordinary day in high school. Casey wasn't sure if he could see how big of a smile covered her face.

"Just passing by for the night?"

"Yeah, you know," he said in a loud whisper, trying to play it off. "Actually, I just dropped my prom date off."

"Really? That's funny, I didn't see you there."

"I think it's funny you're not still there."

"Izzy Jones is the only one in our class who lives around here."

Daniel let out a laugh, then stopped.

"Don't be mean," Casey said.

"I'm not. I just—"

"Izzy actually went to prom."

"What?"

"I said—" Casey stopped in mid-sentence, thinking it was ridiculous for them to be talking like this. "You know—you can climb that big tree over on the side of the house and get up here. That way we won't have to wake my family."

For a second it looked like Daniel might not take her suggestion, then he disappeared and showed up moments later, brushing himself off and walking slowly.

"Good thing you didn't fall and break your neck," she said.

"Good thing you didn't see me climbing up." He laughed, and it was a good sound. "Mind me joining you?"

"I wouldn't have asked if I didn't want you to."

"Yeah, somehow I knew that."

He sat down next to her and stared up at the stars. So far, Casey wasn't sure if he'd even looked at her straight on. At least not since coming up on the roof.

"So aren't you gonna ask?"

"Ask what?" Daniel said.

"Why I'm already home?"

"I'm assuming the place burnt down. Or maybe Liam passed out, though he's never been a big partier. Perhaps they didn't play enough country songs to your liking. Or maybe, just maybe, your date ended up being a dud."

"You're right."

"About your date?"

"Not enough country songs."

When she smiled, she saw him smiling back. This was so strange. Not very long ago, she was slow-dancing with Liam. Now she was sitting down next to Daniel on the roof of her house.

"Why didn't you go? To prom?"

"The girl I wanted to go with already got asked out."

"That's tragic."

"Yeah, it is. That night could've changed her life."

"Maybe it did. Maybe turning you down was the best thing that ever happened to her."

Daniel chuckled. "I've never heard rejection painted in such a positive way."

There was more Casey could have said, both about Liam and about prom, but she didn't want to talk about them. Liam had basically admitted he had no intentions of being "hitched" when he got to college. Thankfully, the moron had shared this before the night was over.

Casey had made sure the night ended there and then.

"So no second-string dates, then?" she asked him.

"Prom is overrated. It's like all those things people hype so much. In the end, they usually end up disappointing you. Unless it's, like, a Springsteen show."

"They played a Springsteen song. I thought of you."

"I can't believe that," Daniel said. "I'm honored."

"That I'm thinking of you?"

"That they played a Springsteen song."

She liked his sense of humor. It was refreshing.

"Music isn't just a hobby for you, is it?" she asked him.

"No. It's a part of me. It's like—like these two hands. Like my ears and eyes. It's like my heart and soul, you know?"

"I love music because it takes me out of the place I'm in. It transports me."

"For me, music is about framing the moment I'm in. It's framed and mounted and then put up on a wall. It's a memory. Every important piece of music in my life has some kind of memory or feeling attached to it."

"What song would be playing right now if you could pick one?"

"Ooh, that's a hard one," Daniel said.

"Anything."

For a few moments, Daniel remained silent. "I can't pick one."

"Then what was the last song playing in your car?"

"That doesn't count."

"What was it?"

"No—I wouldn't call it fitting."

"What was it?" she said, refusing to give up.

"Okay, fine. It was 'Rooster' by Alice in Chains."

"'Rooster'?"

"Yeah."

"Seriously?"

"It was on the radio."

"That's a nice sweet song," Casey joked.

"I told you it didn't fit."

"I can see that in the movie. The boy driving past the girl's house late at night, cranking 'Rooster.'"

She could see the annoyed amusement on his face.

"No, actually, I had the song all lined up to play for you. It's Merle Haggard's "I Think I'll Just Stay Here and Drink.'"

"Ha-ha. Actually, I'm impressed you know Merle Haggard."

Daniel gave her a nod. "I have a lot of musical tastes. Not just rock."

"You're a mysterious, deep sort of guy."

"Ha-ha yourself. No, there's no mystery. Deep, maybe. But no mystery."

"The mystery for me is why you're here," Casey said.

"Really? That's been obvious since the first time I talked to you."

For once, she felt free to say whatever was in her mind and heart. Maybe it was because she felt so safe sitting up on her rooftop. Maybe it was because she knew this guy had good intentions.

"There are a lot of other girls you could've chased this year," she said.

"A lot of them wouldn't have run away so fast," Daniel said. "After all this time, I still don't know what I ever did to make you take off like you do."

"It's not you, it's me. Okay? I won't elaborate, because then I'll suddenly get all down and I already was down before you came."

"You mean I cheered you up?"

"Yep."

"Wow," Daniel said. "There is hope."

"There's always hope. Always."

Dreams

*I*T FELT LIKE they could talk all night long. Daniel forgot about what time it was or that he'd skipped prom earlier or that they were sitting on her rooftop or about anything else except Casey Sparkland. He loved listening to her talk, the way she would shift from one topic to another, always inquisitive and always interesting. She laughed at his stupid little jokes. She also genuinely seemed interested in what he had to say.

"What do you think is up there?" Casey asked, a question that could have been rhetorical or not.

"They say those shiny things are stars."

"The same things that twirl around in your head?"

"Don't give me that."

Casey turned. "What?"

"The dumb jock thing. I'm not a jock. And I'm not dumb."

"Perhaps, but you still have a boy's sense of humor."

"Okay, fine," Daniel said, staring back up at the panorama above them. "I see a million memories."

"How do you see that?"

"Whenever something big happens in my life, I try and find a star to remember it by."

"Does that work?"

He looked at her, thought for a moment, then shook his head. "Nah, not really. Only the big stars. The big memories."

"Like what?"

"They're nothing."

"You've named stars after them. Big ones. They have to be something."

"There's the one on the end of the Big Dipper. See that?"

"I'm awful with constellations."

He moved over and raised his arm above her head so she could see in that direction. "The big one that resembles a spoon."

It took her a few moments but finally Casey saw it.

"That's for my mother."

"What about her?"

"She split when I was in eighth grade."

"Really? What do you mean?"

"She got tired of living with a house of boys. Ran off with another guy."

"I didn't know that," Casey said in a hushed voice.

"I don't talk about it to a lot of people. It torpedoed my dad. He always drank, but now he does so to forget. I guess. I've given up on her ever coming back around, but my father hasn't."

A sigh of wind could be heard in the silent pause. Daniel quickly tried to break it.

"Sorry. The stars don't signify all good memories. Just the ones I can't forget."

"Unlike tonight," Casey said.

"So you're saying this is forgettable?"

"My prom was forgettable. Yes."

"Then what about the rest of the night?"

"I'd prefer to think of this as a new day," Casey said. "I do believe it's past midnight."

"I think that's a good thing to tell yourself. Especially when you danced with one guy at his prom and you're now sitting with another on your roof."

"I didn't exactly invite the other boy up here."

"'The other boy.' That sounds so eighth grade."

"Well . . ." Casey said, looking at him with a playful glance.

"Why is it that this all has to happen now? That I have to be sitting here with you now that the year's almost over?"

"Anybody can win the lottery."

The statement felt so outrageous that Daniel couldn't even believe it himself. Then he thought of it and laughed.

"Too bad I didn't 'win the lottery' a year or two ago."

"You might have spent all the money and ended up broke. That's what Liam did."

"You have a way with words."

"Too bad most boys like video games and action movies instead."

"I'm not like most guys. Especially boys."

"Isn't that what they all say until you realize it's just another line in another sad breakup song?"

"Good point. But I'm not another country song on your CD list, Casey."

"I've grown up listening to country all my life."

"Doesn't mean you can't check out other albums. Doesn't mean you can't try to one day have a star named after you."

Casey nodded, sliding closer to him. She smelled like strawberries. "You're an interesting guy, Daniel Winter."

"And you're an interesting girl."

"How long can interesting last?"

"The Big Dipper is pretty interesting."

"I'd be pretty excited just to make it until the end of graduation."

"So, End-of-Graduation Girl," Daniel said. "What do you want to do after that? After Duke University and all that?"

"I have plans and goals," she said. "I have dreams. I just don't always share them with others."

He could see Casey's bright eyes glancing his way. They suddenly weren't in Asheville or in North Carolina anymore. Daniel felt like they were in their own universe, under unseen stars lighting their little world. He remained quiet, wanting to hear about her dreams.

"I want to stand for something in a world where 'something' means very little. I want to find love that resembles the songs and poems written about it. I want to wake up and wonder what *I'm* going to do and not how I'm going to help some machine become bigger. I want my words to count and mean something. I want to tell some beautiful stories."

"Oh, everybody says that," he said, joking with her.

"It's true."

"Wow," Daniel said. "In your own words, that sounds pretty 'artsy-fartsy.'"

"There's nothing artsy about any of that. I'd love to be a writer but I'll probably end up being an accountant."

"An accountant? Really?"

Casey laughed. "No, I just made that up. I'd be awful at that."

"What would you be good at?" Daniel asked.

"Staring at the stars. Naming them. Dreaming of the stories they could tell."

"That's deep."

"For a high school boy, all of this is pretty deep. Especially after everybody I left was just dancing to the 'Macarena.'"

"You don't give us guys much credit, do you?"

"Don't ever put yourself in that category, Daniel. There are boys and then there's you."

"Should I take that as a compliment?"

"Asking you to come up on this roof was a compliment. The rest . . . well, it's all extra."

"I'll take extra."

"So what are your dreams beyond graduation?" Casey asked.

"I don't know. I mean, I know—I think I know what I want, but I'm not sure. I mean, every time I start thinking about the future I start wondering where I'll be and I promise myself I never want to do anything—like I never want to serve the man, you know? I want to be like you. I just want to do something with the music. If I can. Not to say I'm going to. But I love it and feel like—I feel like it's some burning thing inside. I feel I've got all this *stuff* that just can—that just needs to get out. You know?"

He had been staring up at the stars as he rambled. Suddenly he looked at Casey, who smiled at him in a way he would probably remember the rest of his life.

"What?" he asked, a bit embarrassed, knowing he had been talking too much.

She didn't answer at first, leaving him feeling like he was standing at the edge of that rooftop with nobody to pull him back. Just as he was about to say something to her to break the silence, Casey spoke up.

"Are you gonna kiss me or not?"

The words felt like a falling star, so brief and so surprising. He wondered if he'd really heard them right.

"Okay, so here's the deal," Casey said after he didn't take her invitation and couldn't figure out how to respond. "I like you, Daniel. And after tonight—the whole drama at the prom and the mess afterwards—I didn't expect, well, to be here. With you. But I think—we can talk until morning—I think we have talked till morning. And if it doesn't happen now I don't think it's ever going to happen."

That was enough for Daniel.

He finally did something he wanted to do since the first day of school. He kissed her. This cute firefly of a girl named Casey. This bright falling star.

In that moment, the earth moved and the stars did a loop around his heart and soul.

It was a soft and gentle kiss, but it felt right. It worked. It fit. It felt like a kiss that belonged. He didn't stop and Casey didn't stop either. He could feel her behind the kiss. Not some shy high school girl, but some passionate, original half he suddenly wanted to make whole.

He was the one who broke away, feeling out of breath and a bit dizzy with surprise. He hadn't come to her house expecting this. Or even hoping. He thought maybe, maybe, she might be there and maybe they could talk, but nothing like *this*.

It took him a moment to catch his breath.

"That was the best kiss—" he started to say, but then she kissed him again.

This time the kiss was longer.

Daniel knew there was no way of ever changing course after this night.

Like trying to forget the moon
You always seem to be hanging around
Showing up in the middle of the night
Grinning when the sun goes down.
—Sparkland & Winter, "My Holiday"

PRESENT DAY

Casey Seeks Sanctuary

*W*HY'D YOU EVEN go there in the first place?"

My sister Brittany doesn't quite understand that I'm looking for encouragement and answers, not criticism.

"What if it was Rob and you?"

Brittany, always brutally honest, gave an *as-if* sort of sigh. "If Rob divorced me, I'd never see him again because he'd be at the bottom of a lake."

"Poor Rob."

"Poor nothing," Brittany says. "He knows who he married. Do you know who you married?"

"I thought I did."

"Do you really want to go down this road again, Casey?"

"Oddly enough, right now I'm driving away from him."

"You know what I mean."

"No, of course not."

That's a bit of a lie, to be honest. If I didn't want to have anything whatsoever to do with Burke, then I would have never come back here. Even when he told me I'd inherited a million dollars. I could have put him in touch with my lawyer, or at least a lawyer I'd be hiring. But I didn't because I wanted to express my sympathies and see why I was mentioned in the will and then . . .

And then what exactly, Casey?

"You remember when you came over and cried all night long after he left you for that little tramp?"

"That was a long time ago," I tell Brittany.

"Not by my estimations. A hundred years would still not be long enough."

"I'm not saying I'm going to get back with him."

"That's your history, sis. That's what you do."

"I've been single for several years now."

"You already got back with him once. And how well did that go? And do I even need to bring up that high school loser you went to prom with?"

I should have called Ashley, our youngest sister. She wouldn't have given me any concrete input, but she wouldn't be riding my butt like Brittany here. Emily, another sister, would have been indifferent, which would have been worse. Ashley would make it somehow about herself and her drama, while Emily would feel like I was making a big deal over nothing.

"I never got back with Burke. That was just a night. A mistake."

"I'm talking about the time you thought things were over. When you thought *you* were over."

"That was different. Things were different."

"And what's this, then?" she asks.

"There are some legal reasons I'm here, you know."

"It sounds like you're trying to convince someone. But it doesn't have to be me."

"Be nice," I tell her.

"I'm never going to be nice to that arrogant—"

"Okay," I interrupt, hoping she won't say anything worse than she already has.

"You're staying in Hilton Head, not with him, right?"

"Yes."

"Didn't you go to Hilton Head that one time with—"

"Yes," I interrupt again.

This was a bad idea calling her. *Bad* idea.

"Interesting choice of places to chill out."

I shift in the seat of my car. "I thought you'd be a little more sympathetic considering everything."

"I'm pregnant and my hormones are wacky, so you can't ask for sympathy or empathy."

Brittany and Rob already had a three-year-old son, and like clockwork she was pregnant with their second. I spend a few moments talking about how she's doing. I have to remember my sister is a Sparkland, prone to being overly dramatic.

"I'm moody, cranky, uncomfortable, and hope we're not having another boy," she tells me.

What I would give to be in your shoes.

"But at least I'm not visiting my ex, wondering how to give him his wedding ring back," Brittany adds.

"That's not why I called."

"No? Then why did you call? You surely didn't think I'd give you my blessing."

"I figured I could use some advice."

"Drive far, far away from Burke and his house and his life."

"You really don't like him, do you?"

My sister pauses as she thinks. I see the lines of the interstate that I'm driving on, the rental-car lights cutting through the thick darkness.

"I adored Burke when you two married. Remember? I was one of the ones telling you to go for it. But just because you two look great on a Christmas card doesn't mean you should be together for the rest of your life."

"Rob and you look good together."

"Oh, please. I look like a butterball and Rob is joining me in the out-of-shape department. Burke was the hunky rich guy who managed to woo all of us. I realize I shouldn't have helped send the others away."

"I was the one who picked him, you know."

"We just can't help ourselves, can we?"

"I don't know," I said.

Honestly, I don't.

IT'S EXACTLY TWO songs before I hear one of our songs on the radio. It's strange to be on the road, driving away, and suddenly hearing a song from yesteryear. The simple opening chords give the tune away, and I almost change the radio station. Almost.

It's that easy to suddenly be transported back to the time when I wrote this song with my fellow stargazer and dreamer.

The fact that my last name has been copyrighted several times alongside Daniel's name has always been a great source of pride. I always told him the songs were his, but he wanted them to be ours. He said it was the proper thing to do, but I know deep down he just wanted one more reason to connect with me. He wanted our names to be together, and not just on song lyrics.

I think back to the time Daniel climbed up on my roof and first kissed me, then the happy months that followed.

Did I love him back then?

I'm not sure. It would be easy to say I did, but I don't think I did. I didn't know much about love.

Do you know much now?

The song I'm listening to is the second official song we ever sold. Or that Daniel ever sold. It's called "No More Love Songs," and it was recorded by Sugarland in 2004, a year after our first song came out and two years after I got married. I don't know if Daniel knew it at the time, but it was my attempt to tell him good-bye. It was the most romantic breakup song ever written. So we were told.

"What if all our what-ifs filled the night sky? Brilliant bursts of wheres and untold whys."

Turn it off, turn it off right now.

The song didn't have to be a country song, but since the first song we had written together had been country, the industry wanted another one. Daniel had sent me the tune and I simply filled in the blanks. My lyrics fit the mood and the tone of most of the songs I'd grown up listening to.

"No more rights to all these wrongs. No more tears, no more songs."

My cheeks are already lined with tears before I can wipe them away. I remember writing to Daniel, not in order to get my name on another song, but in order to keep my heart from feeling the big question mark hanging over it. I was a newlywed and yet I still had strange feelings toward Daniel. Writing these lyrics was cathartic.

I realize that in many ways, all of our songs have been a way to say good-bye, in one way or another. There are five of them, though there could have easily been a dozen or more.

If I'd simply gone along for the ride.

Life used to be so easy when I was dumb enough to take things for granted. I wish I could have known a little more and thought through decisions a little more.

"No more words to be said. No more fears, no regrets."

Like a ghost in the night, songs sometimes haunt you when

you least expect them to. They confuse and confound and criticize.

My history would be easy if it only consisted of country songs. But the soul of a rock star ended up coming into my life and interfering with everything.

I drive in the darkness toward the hotel on the beach where I'm hoping to retreat. But something tells me I'm not going to find any answers there. Something tells me I'm simply running away from all the songs I no longer want to hear.

Daniel Seeks Inspiration

*H*EY, POP. IT'S Daniel."

"Daniel? Daniel who?"

It's in morning and I've decided to alert my family that I'm coming back around. Talking to my father in person can be difficult, but trying to talk on the phone can be downright impossible. All because his mind is slowly slipping away.

"Daniel, your son."

"My sons all left me."

The thing with his dementia is that sometimes he can be so nice and charming that it actually makes me like the guy I'm talking with. Other times, it seems to only heighten his meanness.

"Your wife left you," I tell him. "Your sons all live in different places."

"Are you the one without a woman?"

This is like some kind of cruel joke. "Yes, I'm the one."

Dad doesn't have Alzheimer's but rather something that's known as vascular dementia that started after he had his stroke. It's been slowly getting worse. He's insisted on continuing to live in his home, telling us he'd cut ties with all of us if we put him away in a nursing home, which he calls a holding cell.

"I wanted to tell you I'm coming home in a few days. I'm going to be staying for a while."

"And where'm I going?"

He's got a Southern drawl that has the grit of tobacco.

"You're not going anywhere. I'm just going to be staying with you for a while."

"We don't have room for kids."

"Okay, then I'll leave the kids at home."

"Is this Percy?"

I sigh. This could go on for an hour. The strange and sad thing is then he'll get off the phone and forget I ever called in the first place.

"Are you still eating all your meals? Did you have breakfast yet?"

I check in on things like this. Half the time I feel guilty for continuing to pursue my dreams while my father withers away. Philip and Jeff don't have the ability to take care of him. But as for me . . .

"Well, you take care of yourself, okay?"

"Oh, don't treat me like a child," he says as he hangs up.

It doesn't take me long to dial up my brother Philip and tell him the news. I'm curious to ask him if he has any music suggestions, since he lives in Chicago and still fancies himself a hipster even though he is a forty-one-year-old.

"Sorry, you can't steal any more ideas from me," Phil says before even saying hello.

"You said they were free of charge."

"Yeah, that was before I saw them on the show. You actually used them."

"Why do you think I asked for some ideas? You're the one with three kids."

"What? You didn't ask Jeff?"

Our middle brother has one child, and he and his wife are overprotective and trying to shield him from the world. That includes shows like *Dandee Donuts*. Jeff's own words.

"That's funny," I say. "Well, I'd take you guys out for a steak dinner if I wasn't moving back home to take care of Pop."

"What are you talking about?"

I hadn't told any of my family about the job and life situation. They all assumed I was living the good life in Seattle.

"The show fired me."

"Wait—*Dandee Donuts* fired you?"

I laugh. It sounds so pitiful when spoken out loud. "Yeah."

Phil can't help but break out in uproarious laughter. "That's classic. You tell Jeff?"

"You kidding?"

"He's going to be utterly amused."

"Yeah, yeah, I know." This wasn't exactly why I had called.

"So are you really ready to deal with Dad? He's got people who take care of him, you know."

"It seems like the right thing to do. You got room for me at your place?"

"Want to be a full-time babysitter? A nanny? Or a manny?"

"Haha. So hey, your heart still racing from the job? Having hard times sleeping?"

"Oh that's just mean."

"Well you're really not being Mr. Sympathetic."

Phil has a job for a financial company in Chicago and it stresses him out. He and his family have a nice life and don't have to worry about money, but my brother has to worry about his heart. Dad has already had two strokes.

"There's always room for you."

"Good."

"So where are you now?" he asks.

"My last morning in my apartment. Everything I own—everything to my name—is in my car."

"Don't you have a two-seater?"

"Yeah. Pour the salt on the open wound."

This time he doesn't laugh. I guess it hits him now.

"I called because I wanted some music suggestions. Gonna be a long drive. I want to discover some new tunes. I need some inspiration."

"What? Don't have enough songs on your iPod?"

"I have a fresh start. On life. So I figured some new tunes would be cool. Figured you have some new band you're into."

"Oh man, I don't know. Look, I gotta go. Some of us work for a living."

"Give me one musical suggestion."

Of my two brothers, Phil was the one who shared my love of music. Jeff could take it or leave it. Phil and I have spent many long nights talking about and dissecting music. He used to be a big Springsteen and classic-rock guy until moving to Chicago and discovering alternative music. I have gone to several concerts with Phil and his wife, Heidi.

"It's not like I'm going to surprise you with some amazing new group you've never heard of before."

"You might," I say. "I've been busy listening to kids' tunes."

"They really fired you?"

"No, I'm lying."

"That's pathetic."

"The company or my life?"

"Maybe both?"

Once a big brother, always a big brother.

"I hear Kanye West is pretty good," he says, joking again.

"Never heard of him."

He shoots off some names of bands and artists, some I've heard of and a few I'm curious about.

"Hey—maybe you can get the band back together?" Phil says.

Now he's just trying to find any way to cheer me up.

"That would be a disaster. But I am seeing Yaeger before heading home."

"What's he doing now?"

"Serving tables, playing in a band, drinking."

"Ah, the life." He pauses for a moment. "Why don't you come on by before heading down South?"

"You're a bit far away from Asheville."

"Yeah, I know. I can take some time off."

"You never take time off," I say.

"We can picket *Dandee Donuts* on Michigan Avenue."

I think my big brother is softening with age. It's a good thing, because he's been a jerk at times.

"Yeah, maybe I'll come by. We'll see how far I can get."

"Don't be stupid," he says, something he's said before. It's his way of saying be well.

"I SAY THE great song is out there. Go find it. Go write it."

I can hear Harvey's advice and am trying to do exactly that. I've spent the last hour trying to work on a new song, a brand-new, electrifying, and change-the-world sort of tune. Maybe this one last time will be the magical one. At least, that's what I thought. This time, however, it's not just the lyrics that elude me. It's the melody and the chorus and the whole blasted thing.

I go to my computer and seek inspiration. I have a playlist that includes some of the best country songs ever written, according to the experts. Sometimes I listen to these songs just to find some bit of light and hope.

Casey would be laughing at me, knowing I don't like country.

She realizes the irony of having releases in the country-music genre when I've always mocked that category. She once told me "Never say never."

If I could see her, I'd tell her the same thing.

Johnny Cash tells me that love is a burning thing, and I agree. I once tried to get Casey to sing "Ring of Fire" with me, but she refused to play that game. I want to write something like this, but this song—this is holy ground. A simple, heartfelt tune that has this epic backstory. But it also has Cash. I mean—come on.

There's old-school Waylon Jennings. Then there's *really* old-school Jim Reeves.

These songs only make me feel depleted and desperate. Where is my ray of sunshine, my sweet June Carter, when I need her? There are so many things I'd like to say and ask and tell her.

Remember the guy you once fell in love with? This is what I want to ask as Jim Reeves sings "He'll Have to Go."

Remember the guy surrounded by friends? The guy centered in the band? The guy with a party to go to and a place to hang out and people to hitch rides with? This is what I want to remind her of as Taylor Swift sings "Love Story."

Remember all those big ideals and goals and all that bravado? This is what I want to add as Kenny Rogers sings "The Gambler."

That guy is gone. That guy spends a lot of time alone. That guy tends to get bored with the crowds. They make him feel old. They make him feel tired. They remind him of being a kid with ideals and goals and wasted love.

They remind him of you. Like the rest of the world.

I go through a variety of songs and albums but don't find anything that moves me. This is my problem. I need to be moved, and I know who moves me. She's miles away and I'm here in an empty apartment listening to songs booming out of little speakers while strumming my guitar hoping and wishing and praying for greatness. I want to take off these headphones and put on a record instead and crank it up and then slip onto the couch and lock my legs into hers and listen and look and long a bit. Then to give myself over to her.

Maybe then—and maybe unfortunately *only* then—will I find the music in my soul.

Somehow the playlist has turned into something surprising, something I haven't paid attention to, but something that knocks me over. It's Willie Nelson singing "Do Right Woman, Do Right Man." I listen and feel the goose bumps and know that this is the heartfelt sorta stuff I want to create. But again—it's Willie Nelson. He's up there with Johnny Cash and Elvis and Sinatra and all those great classics.

When he starts talking about all the should have beens and could have beens on "Always on My Mind," I want to turn it off. But I can't. I'm stuck.

I need you here to make up the lyrics I'm feeling deep inside. I need your chisel and hammer. I need your shovel. I need your wheelbarrow. I need your hands.

Man, I need a little help.

I'm going to turn off the music and the melodies and all these blasted memories and start driving. I'm going to outrun them.

I'm going to drive fast and try to conjure up some kind of inspiration on this upcoming road trip of mine. Then I'm going to find that one song I've been looking for and deliver it to her front door.

I once dreamed there was a word
That didn't sound absurd
Whenever it was heard
I made this word for you
I'd speak it in your ear
Whenever you were near
Whenever the coast was clear
When it was just us two.
—Sparkland & Winter, "No More Love Songs"

COLLEGE AND DREAMS

(1996–1998)

Summer of '69

SO CASEY SAYS you're going to be attending Blue Ridge Community College?"

Daniel had a mouthful of macaroni pie, so all he could do was nod. That's probably all he would have done anyway, since the question wasn't really a question. More like a grenade tossed into the middle of the Sunday lunch at the Sparkland house. He'd met everybody before, but this was his first time going to church with the ladies and then coming back home to the Sunday meal. They all sat in the dining room around a long, rectangular table that looked as formal as Daniel felt.

He glanced at Casey, who looked visibly annoyed at her mother's question.

"He plays in a group," Casey told her. "That's not exactly something you go to college for."

Daniel wanted to end this conversation as quickly as it had started. He could already tell Mrs. Sparkland didn't like him. She had this cold and stern look about her every time he saw her. It was quite a big contrast to the large, sunny, and smiling portrait of her in the entryway that looked like a shot taken in her twenties. The first time Daniel had come to the door, she opened it and looked at him like he was a rat just crawling out of the garbage. That wasn't exaggerating, either. She asked him if she could help him, as if he were selling skunk fur. Even then, Daniel believed she knew who he was. Casey had surely told her mother he'd be coming over. Since that first time, the icy attitude never seemed to get any better.

At one point that summer, Daniel even mentioned it to Casey. "I think your mother hates me."

"She doesn't hate you," Casey said.

"Every time I show up, she seems to get this look and tone that goes 'Oh, it's *you* again.'"

"No, she doesn't."

"I'm telling you, it's true."

"Mom loved Liam," Casey said. "She loved that we were both going to Duke and that everything was in a nice, neat package. She already had wedding plans made."

"Sorry to get in the way."

Casey had reassured him in her direct and honest style. "Liam was the one who got in the way. He was a jerk. I've told Mom, but she just doesn't see it."

"Do I need to dump you and end up seeing another girl the next day to get her to like me?"

"Liam liked to charm my mother. She's a bit nervous I'm dating a rocker boy."

"Should I be a surgeon? That didn't work out too well for her."

"Ouch," Casey had said, hitting him on the shoulder. "Be nice."

"To your mom?"

"No, to me."

Daniel had, of course, continued to be nice to Casey and her mother and her sisters. He could make the girls laugh. But all the time, Mrs. Sparkland gave him the skeptical evil eye. Sometimes he would try to make her laugh, but she wouldn't even smile. Other times he would say very little but still get a look and feel of resistance from her.

The subject of Daniel's future was off the table until Mrs. Sparkland brought it up again on this Sunday as everybody sat still, wearing what they had worn to church.

"Do you know, Daniel—Casey's father once wanted to be a musician? Before he ended up getting serious with his studies."

"Dad can't even sing," said Emily, the third-born daughter who seemed to have the least amount of humor of any of the girls at the table.

"Nice, Mom," Casey added in a not-so-subtle tone.

It was obvious that Casey had inherited her mother's good looks, but the warmth and charm must've come from her father. Everything about Mrs. Sparkland felt precise, cold, pale. She ate her roast with nice little bites, chewing with nice little chews.

"Well, if I tried being a surgeon, I'd probably accidentally kill someone."

Daniel was just trying to be funny, but only Ashley, the youngest at the table, found it to be so. Casey looked at him with a *shut-up already* look.

This was supposed to be an attempt to get her mother to like him more. They'd only been dating for half the summer. Maybe she'd end up coming around before the summer ended.

As Daniel picked up his fork and noticed the fine china they were using, he wished he could be back home in jeans eating some cereal and watching sports. Then he glanced at Casey and wished she could be there too.

THE ROLLING HILLS of Asheville that had watched the couple all their lives surrounded them on this mid-summer evening. Casey leaned against Daniel as they sat on the stone wall overlooking a canyon below. His rusted-out Camaro behind them blasted Bryan Adams's classic album *Reckless*.

"I'm going to make you love rock music," he told her with his arm clasped around her.

"I don't dislike it. I just prefer something a little slower."

"A little more boring."

She glanced up at him. "Slow doesn't always have to be boring."

"Hmmm. Is that the reason you're making me wait?"

She pulled back and gave him a look. *That* look, the one Daniel recognized as the *you're in trouble* look. The one that said *you better watch yourself, buddy.* It was the same look she had given him in another life when he walked up to her on the first day of their senior year of high school.

"We already discussed that," Casey said.

"I know—I'm just kidding."

"Little jabs like that aren't going to change my mind, Mr. Winter."

"You're a good girl," Daniel said. "You can't blame a guy for thinking like that."

"I most certainly can. But I try not to hold it against you."

Already they felt used to each other, like they'd been together for the last few years. Casey felt like his favorite jean jacket he used to wear all the time until that one night in high school that got him kicked off the football team. Somehow during his drunken blackout, he'd lost his jean jacket somewhere in his oblivion. It had always fit him just right.

"Can you believe summer is almost half over?" she said, changing the subject.

He didn't want to pressure her. Daniel respected Casey's choice to wait, not because she was trying to be a prude, but because it was a choice based on her faith. It was one of the many things he admired about her.

"It feels like it just started," he said.

"There are so many things I have to do before I leave."

"Do them with me. Let me help you do them."

"This isn't like writing a song together," Casey said. "You really want to help me pack?"

"I want to write another song together. Our first was such a hit."

"After you took my advice."

"I took your advice?"

"After about the twentieth time."

Daniel laughed. "Okay, fine, I'm stubborn. I don't like giving up."

"That can be a good thing."

"What do you mean?"

She didn't answer, and for the moment, Daniel didn't understand her. Sometimes Casey was like that. She could be vague one minute and then very specific the next.

The song playing on the car stereo captured the mood and it would be a moment Daniel knew he'd never forget. He knew the power of music, the way a simple song could suddenly stamp itself onto a heart. *That's* exactly what he wanted to do. To come up with something that people would remember. To write a song people couldn't ever forget. To take a moment like this, with this sweet and beautiful girl wrapped up in his arms, and build four splendid minutes around it.

"How do you feel about college?" Daniel asked.

"I'm trying not to think about college."

She moved closer to him and kissed him. Daniel wasn't thinking about college either.

THEY FELT YOUNG and restless and ready for the rest of their lives. High school seemed like a bad storm in the night, and college appeared like a glorious sun almost ready to rise. In between the two, Daniel and Casey found this miraculous thing neither had been looking for: love.

For a moment, it felt like life was on pause and they could relax. They both knew the inevitable was about to happen, that Casey would be leaving and the odds would suddenly be against them. Daniel never let that stop his enthusiasm for her and for them.

Daniel continued to amuse her sisters while he annoyed her mother. Soon he stopped even trying with Mrs. Sparkland, knowing he wasn't Liam and didn't want to ever be a Liam. Casey, on the other hand, charmed his father and made him believe there was hope for Daniel. Hope for something more than playing with three other smelly guys in a band slowly going nowhere. Hope that he would settle down with the right girl who behaved in all the right ways and that might just rub off on him.

Days disappeared and evenings weren't long enough.

"I don't think the night's big enough for Casey Sparkland."

It was little throwaway comments like this that made her love him.

"Is 'Dancing in the Dark' supposed to mean something other than dancing?"

It was funny random comments like this that made him love her.

Daniel loved how Casey could look different every time he saw her. Casey loved how Daniel didn't care how he looked, even though he usually looked so good.

The sun bronzed their skin. Time was no longer a reliable ally. Daniel spent time with his band while Casey got ready for college. She didn't need to work, while Daniel was technically working even if it wasn't technically paying. So both had plenty of time to be around each other and talk about song lyrics and make up song bits.

A couple of blinks, and then the songs were over and they were saying good-bye to each other.

"You're gonna forget all about me," Daniel told her on their last night before she left for Duke for her freshman year.

"No, because I'm going to be coming to see you."

"The university is almost four hours away."

"That means you can get here in almost three and a half driving the way you do."

"You're funny," Daniel told her.

"And I'm not going away."

"Promise?"

"I'll even cross my heart."

"Just don't hope to die. Or date a Duke basketball player."

"Which is worse?"

"I'm a Tarheel fan. You know the answer."

Where Do We Go from Here

"ARE YOU COMING?"

Her roommate was this pretty brunette named Joni. They had their usual crowd they hung out with, and everybody was heading out to a party on this Friday night.

"Yeah, I'll be there in a minute."

Casey and Daniel had talked about this. They each had lives to live. They weren't married or engaged. Neither of them wanted to be pining after the other on a Friday night, feeling lonely and confused and jealous. Yet it had been several days since she had heard from Daniel and she was growing concerned.

Don't worry about the boys in this town, her mother had told her last time they spoke. *You're going to meet some nice young men at the university.*

Casey had taken note just how her mother called guys in the town "boys" while she called them "nice young men" at Duke.

I've met some not-so-nice young devils, Mom.

Casey had hoped Daniel would call before she ended up heading out. Her message earlier even told him she was heading out, so he should try to call before nine. It was quarter after nine and she was feeling antsy and curious.

The phone in her hand felt like some bomb that might go off.

Give him another call.

But she didn't want to appear desperate. He was just busy. That was all. He usually called once a day, but maybe this was a tough week.

Call his home just to see if he's okay.

But she didn't want to burden Daniel. He still lived with an overbearing father who did that enough. Casey wasn't about to be the mother Daniel never had. He needed to figure out on his own what he would be doing with his life.

Another statement from her mother stuck out in her head: *Don't be naïve and think your future's waiting for you back here.*

Of course, her mom had been referring to Daniel. Casey had thought of a nice comeback but decided against reminding her mother that she had met Dad at Duke.

It would be so nice to hear his voice. Just to get a nice, healthy dose of Daniel before going out and seeing all the upperclassmen acting like God's gift to women everywhere. It had only been three months since school had started, but those three months had felt so long at times. She couldn't wait for Thanksgiving to come, and then for Christmas break, just to see Daniel again and spend some more time with him.

One more minute.

"Casey?"

This was exactly what they had said they *wouldn't* do. She didn't want to be that girl, the one with the boyfriend, always waiting and wondering and talking about some ghost from afar. She didn't want her identity to be wrapped around some guy who wasn't even there.

"I'm coming."

If Daniel called, he could do what she'd been doing the last few days and leave a nice voice mail.

THAT NIGHT AS she walked back to her room with Joni, they laughed about the odd characters they'd met at the party. And they couldn't stop talking about the not-so-odd football player who had introduced himself to both of them.

"I think he's totally into you," Joni said.

"Please."

"He was."

"You told him I have a boyfriend."

"Exactly. And it worked like a charm."

"What do you mean?"

"He's the starting quarterback of the football team. He gets to pick who he goes out with."

"No he doesn't," Casey said. "Not if it's me."

"Ooh. Playing hard to get."

"I'm not available to *get*."

They were tired and slap-happy and the way Casey snapped back and said the word "get" made Joni crack up, which made Casey do the same. Joni had one of those infectious laughs so loud you couldn't help but join her.

"You're not married, are you?"

"No," Casey told her roommate once they were back in their room.

"Isn't your boyfriend missing?"

"He's not missing. He doesn't have to check in with me."

"So call him."

"Daniel?"

Joni shook her head. Obviously she was talking about the starting quarterback they'd met.

"No way," Casey said. "I don't have his number."

"He gave it to me."

"Maybe he likes you."

Joni shook her head and she took her hair down. "No way. He likes you."

Her roommate handed her the piece of paper with the number.

"Burke Bennett?" Casey asked when she saw his full name. "Come on. Sounds like a politician or a banker."

"Or a hunky quarterback. With money."

"How do you know he has money?"

Joni shook her head. "I pay attention."

Casey put the piece of paper on her desk and then noticed her answering machine. She had a message. From Daniel.

All she could do was sigh.

Do You Feel Loved

*T*HEY HAD STAYED in and avoided the crowds and endured Daniel's father and watched the ball in New York drop and had spent a long time kissing each other after it did. This was their first New Year's Eve together, and soon this dream would be gone and classes would be back in session. Neither of them had wanted to talk about that, though. Neither of them wanted the night to end.

Daniel was the first to bring up the issue after listening to Casey tell another story about one of her roommates. They lay on the old couch in a room that smelled like onions. Daniel had made them all spaghetti earlier. It was either enduring his dad and onions in a cramped space or fighting off Casey's mother and her sisters in a less private place. Daniel knew his father would be out by this time of night anyway.

"I can tell you miss them," he said.

"Yeah, sure."

"You miss school."

"I didn't say that," Casey said.

"It's okay to admit it."

"It's fun, but this is fun too. I had a really great Christmas break."

"Christmas dinner was a bit awkward."

"At least some of my relatives were nice," Casey said. "I'm so glad you didn't meet my father's girlfriend."

"Yeah, I'm really disappointed too," Daniel joked.

"I'm sure you miss your classes."

He moved so he could look at her in the dim light. He'd been sitting behind her, Casey wrapped up in his arms and legs as they watched '96 change a digit. Now he wanted to face her.

"I dread the thought of going back."

"I still don't know why you're even going to school."

"That's nice to know."

"No, you know what I mean," Casey said. "I'm talking about your music. Why are you putting it on hold?"

"I never said I'm putting it on hold. I'm doing the right thing."

"Are you sure?"

Daniel felt a bit defensive. "Well, you're one to talk, Miss English Major."

"What do you mean?"

"I thought you wanted to be a poet."

Casey laughed, looking away at the television for a moment. "I'd also like to eat."

"Yeah, well, me too."

"People can still make a career out of music. Some can be really successful."

"And you're sayin' you can't?"

"I don't see many full-time successful poets, do you?"

"Snoop Dogg?"

Daniel was joking, but Casey took this and ran with it. "That's my point exactly. A musician. A very successful one too."

"So you're going to teach and give up writing?"

"I'm a freshman," Casey said in an almost exasperated tone. "I have a little time left."

Daniel leaned over and kissed her again. It never got old.

"Do you think it can really happen?" he eventually asked her.

"What?"

"This. You and me. Us. Do you think we can last?"

"Of course I do."

"Do you really?" he asked Casey. "I mean *really*. Be honest."

"When am I not honest with you?" she said. "What? Are you having second thoughts or something?"

Daniel shook his head, touching the outline of her soft cheek. "I just see us having to work really, really, really hard. Even then, who knows what will happen?"

"So we work really, really, really, *really* hard on this. On us."

"Makes me feel tired."

She snuggled up to him. "Makes me feel warm."

"I hate being away from you wondering what you're up to."

"I'm right here."

"Right now. But soon you'll be—"

"Shhhh," she said, reaching up and putting a finger against his lips.

"You know I love you, Casey Sparkland?"

"I do."

"How do you know?"

"Because you waited all that time before finding me sitting on my rooftop."

"I keep driving by but you're never there now," Daniel joked as he tightened his grip around her.

"Don't ever stop checking to see if I'm there. Okay?"

"Promise."

ONE MARCH NIGHT found Daniel in that same old house on that same old couch cursing at his father and his life. He'd come home from playing at a local bar with his band only to find his father choking on his own vomit. Thankfully Daniel had come home when he did.

Wasn't it supposed to be the opposite, with Daniel being the one stumbling around drunk and throwing up? His pop barely acknowledged him and even asked if he was still wasting his time playing music. Daniel had wanted to ask his father if he was still wasting his life drinking beer.

That was the first night Daniel wanted to leave. He wanted to get out of that place and never look back. A part of him felt chained to it because of his father, but that wasn't the only reason. Casey had a big part in that too. A huge part.

Daniel knew he needed to see Casey again. And soon, before the shadow of this life felt too large to crawl out from underneath.

He needed to see Casey again to get rid of those shadows.

"CAN I STEAL you away for a week?" he said to her on the phone.

So it began.

She had just come back from a morning class and got this unexpected call from Daniel, whom she hadn't spoken to in a couple of days.

"What do you mean?" Casey asked.

"I mean spring break is coming up and I want to take a break with someone who reminds me of springtime."

"If I didn't know you, I'd say that might be one of the best lines I've ever heard."

"Too bad I can't come up with them for lyrics," Daniel joked.

She glanced at the stack of textbooks on her desk. "You know—I'm a good girl, and you're considering dropping out of college after your first year."

"You love me for the dreams in my heart."

"I love you for having dreams to begin with."

"I thought it was for my rock-hard abs.

"Well, yes, I love your sense of humor too," Casey said.

Always a quip, always a comeback. They made a good team because this could go on and on and on.

"I'm serious. You have until two this afternoon."

"Wait—what? To decide?"

"To leave."

So it started.

Casey surely knew he was serious. She decided in that moment.

"Okay," she told him.

Yes, she had a day and a half worth of classes left, but she never skipped, and she also never got offers like this. Those classes and those books could wait. The guy at the other end of the phone—she didn't want him waiting.

Hours later, when he saw her with a duffel bag over her shoulder, Daniel gave her a big grin.

"You made a good choice," he said as he entered her dorm room.

"We better leave before I find my sanity and change my mind."

NOT ALL KISSES are made equal.

Sometimes they can sway and swagger, like a playful kiss on someone's list.

Sometimes they can be sweet and sincere, the kind that make you alter your life and your destination and go in another direction. The kind often compared to a rose, so delicate and so beautiful.

Sometimes you have a kiss to build a dream on.

Sometimes they're simply kisses you can't stop talking about.

Yet it was midnight, and Casey found herself twirling and

swirling on a dance floor as the singer said she didn't have to be rich or cool or any of that other stuff.

There weren't many clubs like it in Hilton Head but it didn't really matter where they were. It was their first night there and they went out on a whim. Daniel was dancing to Prince and looking like a reject from a high school musical. His moves were off and his arms were moving and there was nothing sexy at all about that white man dancing like a hyena. And yet, she'd never wanted this guy in front of her more than she did right then. Simply because he didn't care. He was just trying to make her smile.

"Act your age, not your shoe size," Daniel mouthed the lyrics to the song as he wiggled and moved his chin back and forth in front of her.

"Oh dear."

He spun her like a princess. Then finally they came together again and they kissed. And it was the crazy, hilarious moment when Casey knew this was the guy, this was the insane person she wanted to spend her life with.

This first year away had been harder than she thought, but if they'd made it up to now, who's to say they couldn't make it last?

She decided she wanted her life to be this out of breath and out of touch and happy and warm.

She wanted all of those kisses and more.

THEY HAD SPENT three days together on Hilton Head Island. Full, carefree, and fabulous days where time dripped off like sweat beads on the beach. It was nighttime and they held each other on the sand and watched the sleeping Atlantic Ocean in front of them. That was the moment Casey knew she was ready. The moment she had waited for. So far there hadn't been any pressure from Daniel. They had stayed together but he'd slept on the couch.

Casey didn't want to wait, not anymore. She had waited long enough.

"No."

It wasn't the response she expected from Daniel.

He held her with his arms and legs wrapped around her like a warm blanket. "It was my slick dance moves, wasn't it?"

She knew he wouldn't believe it even if she told him the truth. "Oh, definitely," she said in a joking manner.

For a while neither of them said anything. The shores of their tranquil setting felt like another world and another life to her. She had been there before, but never like that, never feeling so adult and so free. They could do anything they wanted to do.

"I don't want you regretting something we do tonight a month from now. Or a year from now," Daniel said.

"I'm ready."

"No."

"I don't get it," she said. "After all this time—you've told me you want this—"

Casey assumed after all this time—after being away from Daniel and occasionally arguing about the distance and the time apart—Daniel would want to. She didn't understand.

"Because this—all of this—is like some fairy tale," Daniel told her. "This isn't real. This is make-believe. The sun and the sand

and yes, my sweet dance moves. Let's make this the highlight of the trip. Being here, together. Not worrying about something we may or may not want to talk about tomorrow."

She gripped his arms. "I want to stay here forever."

"Me too. But that's the problem. You'll wake up realizing that might not be the best idea."

"I don't make any decisions unless I'm ready."

"I don't want to be a mistake in your life," Daniel said. "You know what I want. But not like this. I promised you—I promised. And I'm sticking with my word."

"I'm not sure if I can handle such a gentleman."

He laughed. "One day, hopefully, you will have to. And you'll see just how gentle I can be."

There wasn't anything else that needed to be said. Not that night. Not in that moment.

THE NEXT DAY, it took them half an hour to write the song. It was a melody that Daniel had carried around with him for a while. He added a chorus and then let Casey write the words. It was a sweet love song called "My Holiday."

Daniel didn't have to wonder who the lyrics were written about.

ON THE WAY home, as Daniel drove the car and Casey thought about the spontaneous spring-break trip, she slipped her hand into his and then leaned over to kiss him on the cheek.

"What's that for?" he asked.

"For being you. Don't ever change."

"You sure about that?"

She leaned over and stared up at him. He didn't want to avoid looking at her, yet he had a road to focus on.

"I want you to promise me something, Daniel Winter."

"What's that?"

"Don't ever give up on your dreams. Don't. They're what make you you."

He couldn't help the smile that stretched out over his face. "Only if you promise me the same."

"I don't have dreams."

"Yes, you do. They're more honorable than mine."

"What are you talking about?" Casey asked. "You know exactly what you want and where you want to go. You have this passion."

"So what about you, then? Where do you want to end up?"

"Wherever you're going."

It was hard to resist an answer like that coming from a girl like Casey.

"Okay—I promise I'll never give up on my dreams if you don't give up on yours," he told her as he touched one side of her gentle cheek.

Casey kissed him. "Deal."

Hungry Heart

$\mathcal{I}$T HAD BEEN a couple of months since he'd seen Mrs. Spark-land. But he knew there was no way of avoiding her that morning, since she was sitting near the exit to the Starbucks. The last time Daniel had seen her was in August, right before Casey went back to school. He didn't spend a lot of time at her house simply because he still got the looks and the vibe and the small undermining comments from Casey's mother. Yet he'd helped Casey get ready to go back to Duke.

As he started heading toward the door holding his cup of coffee, he stepped over and said "Hello, Mrs. Sparkland" in a very polite and friendly manner.

She obviously had seen him, because she gave him a serious smile and said hello, and then said, "Why don't you have a seat for a moment, Daniel?"

There was something in the way she said this that made Daniel think it wasn't a question but rather a command. He nodded and then slid into the leather chair right next to Mrs. Sparkland.

I wish I'd done something with my hair this morning.

It was eight and he didn't have any classes to go to. He was practicing with his band and starting to play regular gigs as well as working a job at a hardware store. Those were temporary things before, well, before whatever happened next happened.

The morning light made Mrs. Sparkland look even more pale than usual. She wore designer jeans and a designer T-shirt like someone much younger. Her hair was pulled back but there was no mistaking the wrinkles on her face.

"Daniel, you really are a cute kid," she told him in a tone he hadn't heard before. She wasn't trying to suggest something and wasn't being cynical. It sounded like a sincere comment, even though it made him feel about five. "You're a nice boy, and I can understand Casey's infatuation with you. But wouldn't you agree with me that eventually, we all have to grow up?"

If Daniel had had a mouthful of coffee, this would have been the moment he'd spit it out all over himself. Thank God for hot coffee that needed to cool.

"Yeah, I guess," he answered, which was really a nonanswer.

Mrs. Sparkland leaned over as the forced smile still remained on her lips. "Do you see a future with my daughter?"

"Yeah, I do."

"And you see a future with this music thing of yours?"

This music thing.

It sounded like he'd invented a little motorcycle for hamsters that he was trying to sell.

It's music, the thing that drives this world and makes soulless people like you even try to feel. It's the backdrop of our lives and the soundtrack of our hearts.

"Yeah, I want to do something with music."

He felt paralyzed, unable to articulate exactly what he wanted to say. This was an adult—but more than that, this was Casey's mother. He didn't want to—he *couldn't*—say something like what the voices going through his head were saying. If there was ever to be a future with Casey, he didn't want some awful comment he made hanging over his head like a broken halo.

"I can understand why Casey likes you. You know, deep down, she's always wanted to be a poet. Not a writer—not a journalist or a novelist, but a poet. And I've always told her that it was great for her to keep a journal and write down her thoughts and feelings, but those were for her bedroom. Those didn't belong in the real world. Someone doesn't make it in the real world writing poetry."

"I'm still waiting to see if I'm getting into surgeon school," Daniel said.

He couldn't resist. He wanted to say more, lots more, but he held off.

Mrs. Sparkland leaned back and took a sip of her coffee from a large glass mug. She stared at him for a moment.

She really loathes me.

"Every girl eventually has a Daniel Winter in their life. Sometimes, if they're lucky, they give them up. I had one. I wouldn't have this life if I'd let him linger around."

Daniel wanted to ask Mrs. Sparkland about her failed marriage, and whether "this life" that she referred to was really what she wanted. He wanted to ask how she could judge him in this way.

But mostly, he wanted to ask how in the world someone so special could come from someone so cruel.

Instead, he simply said, "Well, it's been nice seeing you."

"Take care of yourself," Mrs. Sparkland said, as if she might never see him again.

CASEY FOUND DANIEL outside the frat house standing on the sidewalk. She wondered how long he'd been standing there. The music from behind them still blasted through the cool midnight air.

"Where'd you go?"

"I was wondering the same thing as I was talking to some meatheads," Daniel said. "So this is how you spend your weekends at Duke, huh?"

"Stop. You'd fit in with all of them. Don't start sounding like some *artiste*."

Daniel laughed and rolled his eyes as if he had some kind of story.

"What is it?" Casey asked.

"Nothing. I'm just tired."

"Since when have you been tired around midnight? And when have you wanted to leave a party? Back home I'd be the one wanting to leave."

"That's back home."

Casey slipped in front of him and forced him to stop. "What's up?"

"Nothing."

Their time at Hilton Head felt like ten years ago. Somehow, the university felt too small and Asheville felt too far away. It was 1997, more than a year since they had graduated from high school, and several months since they'd seen each other over the summer.

"Don't do this," Casey said.

He shook his head and looked away. Students passed them by, wondering if they were fighting or about to kiss. She tried to ignore them.

"You're not telling me something," Casey said.

Daniel brushed his hair back and she noticed it was getting pretty long. He was staring up at the sky as if he wanted to tell her something.

Maybe this is the moment.

It was November and the holidays were approaching and sophomore year would be coming to a break and . . .

We've made it this far.

Sometimes Casey would wonder what she was doing with him. Then he'd show up and kiss her and remind her.

Sometimes Casey knew this couldn't ever be anything more. But the feelings inside of her, they sometimes scared her, because they were turning into something more. They were beginning to be solid and heavy and thick like impenetrable stone.

"Daniel?"

"I'm moving to New York," he said. "I've got to. I swear, if I'm around here—not *here,* not this campus, but North Carolina—if I stay here, I'm going to end up in an early grave."

"What's going on?" she asked.

"Everything. My father, for one. I just can't deal with him anymore. He needs to be put in a rest home or something. I'm not a caretaker. And with my music. And my band. It's time. And I don't care if anybody says it's just silly and stupid, because it's time. I'm going to do this thing."

She tried to capture his gaze and attention. "Hey—look at me. I hope you're not talking to me, because I know that. I've been telling you for a while you should do something like this."

Daniel nodded. "Yeah, I know."

"So that's good news, right?"

"I don't know what kind of news that is. At least—for us."

She took his hands into hers and leaned over and kissed him. She could tell he tried to resist it but then he let go.

"We'll figure things out, okay? But we'll do it together. Okay?"

Daniel smiled and nodded.

"Come on," Casey said. "Let's get away from the noise. Maybe you can serenade me tonight."

★   ★   ★

IT WOULD BE some random, passing thought uttered out loud. So many of them are, and they get ignored and overlooked. Yet Casey didn't ignore or overlook this particular one.

"All I want really is just to be able to write that perfect song," Daniel said. They were driving and had just heard one of those magnificent songs that got played often. It was during Thanksgiving break, while Casey was back home in Asheville spending some time with family and with Daniel.

This statement wasn't something unique or profound. Daniel said stuff like this all the time. But it came when she was so busy at school, and so curious about the future, and so hesitant about the two of them.

Daniel, on the other hand, was only really focused on one thing. On one very particular thing.

It made Casey nervous. Really nervous.

THE NEW GUITAR was the final straw.

"Casey, I can't . . ."

Daniel held a Martin guitar in his hand and knew that she had spent a lot—too much—on this Christmas gift.

"Where did you find this?"

"It's used."

"Well, yeah," Daniel said, strumming it and hearing the classic sound of the acoustic guitar. "This is a Martin. This is like—way, *way*, too much."

"I got a good deal," she told him with a smile.

It was late Christmas Eve and they were downstairs in the finished basement. Thankfully Mrs. Sparkland had gone to bed and Casey's sisters were leaving them alone.

Something about this gift that Casey couldn't wait to give him made him sad.

I can't give her anything in return except the promise that my dreams might end up coming true.

"What's wrong?"

"Casey, I . . ."

He couldn't watch her settle for less in her life. He didn't want to weigh her down. He didn't want her to be stuck behind because of him.

"I can't accept this."

"Yes you can. Why not?"

"Because I can't give you anything in return."

She held up her gold necklace already around her neck. "I told you I love this."

"No, I'm not talking about that. I'm talking about us. I'm talking about the fact that—that you're always going to be coming back here. You always have to turn back around to see what I'm up to. Coming back home to see Daniel."

"What's gotten into you?"

He shook his head. "I think we need to take a break."

"What? Why?"

"I'm moving to New York."

Casey looked perplexed and tried to understand what he was saying.

"Look—your mother said this herself not long ago when I ran into her. I'm holding you back. You don't have to be tied to me or to Asheville or to some nice idea of teen love."

Now Casey looked angry. "What are you talking about? What'd my mother say to you?"

"Nothing."

"No, you tell me."

"She's just being protective of her little girl."

Casey shook her head and stood up for a moment. Daniel had to pull her down and sit her back on the couch. "Don't. Just—please, Case, don't. It's not just that."

"Are you dating me or dating my mother?"

The Christmas tree in the corner of the room, one of three trees in the house, glowed in white, glittering lights. This wasn't how Daniel imagined the night turning out. But seeing that guitar and knowing what it meant somehow broke him.

I need to prove I'm worthy of it, but I can't tell her that.

"Do you want to 'take a break'?" Casey asked.

"I saw what your life's like at Duke. I didn't fit in there. You're so happy with all your friends and all your fellow Dukies."

"Don't."

"I've been miserable being back here waiting for life to show up. I need to try and do something with myself. I need to follow my dreams."

"And in order to do that, you have to throw me to the curb?"

Daniel shook his head. He wanted to explain to her how he felt, but *he* still wasn't sure how he felt.

He just didn't deserve to be in that house sitting next to her holding on to that guitar and living in that life. He felt like he needed to get somewhere before sitting next to her.

But Casey doesn't feel that way, you dimwit.

"Daniel, talk to me."

"I don't want you waiting around for me. I don't want—" He put the guitar on the couch next to her. "I don't want you waiting for the time and the place when I finally deserve a gift like this."

"Stop it. You deserve it now. That's what a gift is."

Daniel felt confused and tired and mostly depleted.

"So give me another gift then," he asked Casey. "Give me some time. Give me some time to figure things out."

She didn't understand and didn't act like she wanted to understand. "If that's what you want," Casey said.

I don't know what I want, but I know I don't want to hold you back. From anything.

"I WANT TO take you somewhere," Daniel told her.

Casey was about to go back to school and hadn't expected to see Daniel again. She didn't want to see him, yet now that he asked her to go somewhere, part of her wondered if he was going to change his mind. About her and about them. She wasn't sure how this was supposed to work—about giving him "time."

He stood by her doorway and he actually didn't seem worried a bit about her mother showing up. Casey half expected some big, brutal farewell, but instead she saw his eyes. Blue and whimsical and up to something. The old Daniel was back. The one who seemed to have disappeared lately was back.

"Where do you want to go?" she asked.

"Somewhere you've never seen."

"How do you know?"

"Because I've asked."

"Daniel—"

"Look, I know the way I've been. I think life and my father and *your* mother have all been getting to me. But that's not your fault. It's just—well, just trust me and get in the car."

She had been up all night thinking of everything she wanted and needed to say. In the morning she would be going back to Duke and she knew the good-bye that night might be the forever kind. Whatever their "break" meant, she knew well enough that it was a breakup. Daniel might never come back around again.

So if this is good-bye, at least he's in a good place to say it.

She climbed in the car, unsure where he was going to take her, unsure of how she would respond.

Moments later, they stood on top of Grandfather Mountain. She had heard of it all her life and had seen pictures of it but had never stepped foot up on it until now. They were 5,946 feet above sea level on the rocky peak, surrounded by other climbers and tourists.

"Why'd you bring me here?"

The wind didn't do anything to Daniel's already-messy hair. He brushed it back like an explorer reaching new lands. "I wanted you to see something you knew was there with your own two eyes. I wanted you to see and feel it and know it's real."

Rolling hills stretched out on all sides of her.

"I never thought it wasn't real."

"There are other things, Casey. Things you know can and should be. Things that are real. Places you don't want to go. Scenes you don't want to see."

For a moment, she shut her eyes and said his name. When she opened them, they were full of tears.

"I told you this was going to be hard," she said.

She had made up her mind and didn't want to backtrack. She didn't want to try to convince him. She especially didn't want to have to hurt him.

Daniel shook his head and held her hands. "This isn't about you and me. We happened. We have each other and will always have each other. I don't know what tomorrow holds for me. I might be passing by your house in the middle of the night and find you back up on that rooftop. Who knows. All I know is that there are things inside of you—inside your heart and soul—that are there for a reason. Don't settle for less. Don't settle for second place. Don't settle for not soaring this high in life, Casey. Do not settle. Don't. Regardless if I'm around or not. Don't settle."

Before they were to go back down the mountain and leave each other's lives, Daniel held her one last time. Then he looked down at her, this sad smile on his face, and he asked her the question.

"Are you?"

"Am I what?" Casey asked, not understanding.

"Gonna kiss me?"

She smiled. Even then, as they were saying good-bye, he could make her laugh.

"Maybe not," she teased.

"Well, I had to try."

Casey kissed him one last time, knowing it would most likely be the last kiss they ever shared.

For a moment, standing on top of that rock, the kissing couple was alone and together and they were going to last. They looked and felt and acted like they could possibly last. But then Casey broke away, and the moment was gone, and the kiss was over.

What if all our what-ifs filled the night sky
Brilliant bursts of wheres and untold whys.
—Sparkland & Winter, "No More Love Songs"

PRESENT DAY

Daniel Deals with the Past

I'M NEAR A midway point in this cross-country drive back home, this journey toward finding the song I've been looking for. I'm close to Colorado and contemplating contacting an old acquaintance.

So far, the letter I sent to Casey hasn't gotten a response. I wonder if she's even read it, and if she does, if it will mean anything. Then I think of the last voice mail I left with my agent and wonder when he'll get back to me about a specific time to meet.

I listen to a song through the open window of my car. The song sounds like the name of the band: Fun. I remember laughing when I first heard their name, but the more I've thought about it,

I've thought how clever the name is. It's perfect. Sometimes simple works best. Sometimes you overthink things when you get older. Like love, for instance.

Young love is like a gloriously overproduced, overhyped pop song. So fun to dance to in the dark, taking your breath away, only to be forgotten when the sun rises. The lyrics can feel deep but seem to disintegrate when examined closely. You will always remember it with fondness when you're older and wiser but you will know better.

I think this as I glance at the rugged Rocky Mountains from the parking lot. I lean against my car eating an Arby's sandwich and letting the sun share a little vitamin D. If it wasn't so clear and hot I wouldn't know the date or the month. It feels like I've been in hibernation around, oh, maybe half a decade or more. I think of all those *Dandee Donuts* songs I made up and think about all the wasted time and energy.

Chances are, I won't hear from Casey. Chances are, our story is already over and has been for some time. My short and sweet little note will mean nothing to her. Maybe her mother will open it and then burn it. I had my chance and I said no. She might even say I said no twice, which is funny because all I seem to remember is her telling me no and no way and not going to happen.

I finish the sandwich and then find my iPhone, scrolling through it with greasy fingers to look at some photos I haven't seen in a while. I'm close to Denver, close to a piece of my past, close to something I still haven't fully dealt with. Then I see them. The engagement shots.

The girl I almost married. The woman I never really fell in love with but really, honestly tried to.

Sheryl Miller. The athlete who tried to whip me into shape and almost managed to capture my heart as well. Almost.

Sheryl is tall and toned like some kind of Olympian. She said she had a choice whether to train seriously to try to make the Olympic swimming team. That's how good she was at her sport. She was also smart and decided to get her master's in something to do with math. Yeah, that's how much I paid attention to Sheryl talking about academics. I dropped out of college after my sophomore year, so what did I know? Sheryl intimidated me, to be honest, with abs I'd never personally achieve in my life and an IQ probably double mine. But I guess she liked music too, and that's where we found common ground.

Sorta like someone else, right?

I boarded the speedboat named Sheryl and got far off land and far out to sea and I think I was blinded by the sunlight of her life. Gorgeous and smart, yes. Our engagement pictures, the half dozen I still have, make us look like some winning, happy couple. We were, until that one night I ended things. Thankfully it was months before the wedding, a date we had yet to set due to the question marks I held in my heart.

I sigh. These little reminders are painful, yet still aren't something I can seem to part with.

It's been a year and a half since I last saw Sheryl. I want to go back and see her and apologize. The last time I said good-bye, I told her I'd see her very soon. That had meant weeks, maybe a month. It's amazing how a few weeks can morph into a couple of years so easily, like the simple blink of an eye and the slow exhale of a breath.

I flip through the pictures, and then I see one I haven't seen for a while. A shot of Casey at a concert. The same summer I proposed to Sheryl.

Not everything in life has to balance itself out or add up, but in my case, the one set of pictures featuring Sheryl exists because of this one of Casey. Yet that's a slow track on the second side of an album that hasn't been played for a long time. Nobody plays albums anyway, do they?

Thirty-five years old and so incomplete, like a record collection missing all the B's, like the Beatles and the Bee Gees and the Beach Boys.

What a travesty that would B.

"THE WORST MOMENT on the worst day was the start of something new and wonderful."

Sheryl says this and I feel like running away. I haven't felt this awkward in years.

Maybe it's a good thing to have calls and letters ignored.

I took a chance since I was near Denver to reach out and see if Sheryl was around. Now I'm dining with her.

"I realized I'd run away from what I once believed in, from what I had grown up hoping for. God spoke to me and I knew I needed to run to Him."

I nod and smile as Sheryl talks, but this feels painful.

"And the moment—the very second almost—that I ran to Him—that's when I met Blake."

It's funny she mentions Blake, because he's sitting on my right side at this tapas restaurant, eating like she's talking about the new superhero movie just released.

"I knew that all things work out for the best. I was blinded because for a while I'd been trying to do my own thing, and that included you."

"Usually people equate me with the devil," I say, trying to make a joke, but I feel no sort of humorous response, especially from Blake.

Blake looks like the guy I imagined Sheryl would marry. The fact that she's married and they're both here and she's talking about me in this open and honest way makes me get a bit resentful. I act like I'm fine and I'm happy and life has never been better, but inside I'm feeling a bit jealous. Not really because Blake got Sheryl. I think I'm jealous that Sheryl got someone as great as Blake.

He's the type of guy who probably will never have to worry about love handles. The kind who probably jogs with Sheryl and then gives her back massages. I bet he cuts up things to stir-fry in the kitchen in that fast and natural way the chefs do on television. He looks like the host of one of those food shows on Bravo, good-looking and smiley and totally looking like someone who never, ever eats all the food they cook on the shows.

I was born not to like this guy but I can't help it because, of course, Sheryl mentioned my love of Bruce and Blake mentions that he saw Bruce in concert the last time he came around. Did I? Of course not. Those little *Dandee Donuts* songs weren't quite paying the bills. I think Sheryl mentioned what Blake does but I think I buried that info, the same way I'm going to bury the memory of this night.

Great idea to come by and make sure Sheryl has moved on.

We share the little plates of tapas, which resemble something coming out of a kids' meal at McDonalds. Just a bit fancier. Maybe Blake's going to reach over and hand me a toy in a plastic bag.

Sheryl never asks me how my love life is going, or how my career is going, or how my faith journey is going. They're all on a similar path. I could draw it out for her if we were at a place that had paper instead of linens over the table. I could draw her three descending lines, spiraling down.

"I'm so glad you called us," Sheryl says, smiling, never happier, never more content.

I want to take a fork and plunge it into my gut. Instead, I smile and raise my eyebrows.

It's funny, because I really thought I called just her.

I ALWAYS USED to hate it when a couple in a movie would be content letting the girl go out and have a drink or a cup of coffee with an old flame. I'd think, *Yeah, they're so content that nobody questions whether anything will happen.* In this case, however, getting some Starbucks alone with Sheryl really truly doesn't mean anything.

"You were pretty quiet at dinner." Sheryl states the obvious.

"A lot going on with you two."

"I noticed you showed up by yourself."

"I left my Peruvian wife in the car."

"Very funny."

"There's only me. That's all."

Sheryl and I sat in comfortable chairs in a busy Starbucks in downtown Denver. She took a sip from her cup and turned her head, looking as if she was trying to examine me to see what was wrong.

"Still looking for that perfect inspiration?" she asks.

"Not really. I've tried to set the bar a little lower. I'm hoping for just a warm body next to me at bedtime."

"She's out there. I believe that."

I can't help laughing. "I came here thinking you might need closure. Seems like I'm the one who needs it."

She puts a hand on mine. "You're right. But I'm not the one you need it with."

It's crazy how adult she seems, how far she's moved on. She hasn't just moved on down the road but she's out state and out of mind.

"Is it that obvious?"

"It was obvious when I first met you," Sheryl says. "I had hoped I could try and make you forget about her, whoever she might be. I thought I could outperform the others, like it was some race I was swimming. But I realized you were still stuck at the blocks and hadn't ever even gotten into the water."

"I thought this might be a whole lot more dramatic."

"Still looking for that perfect song?"

Somehow Sheryl is making fun of my soul. I just don't know how I let her inside it.

"That's mean."

"You are, aren't you?" Her eyes make me feel naked and naïve.

"I have been since I was sixteen."

"That's the thing with this world, Daniel. There is no perfect song. There is no perfect anything. You know that, right?"

"'Born to Run' is pretty close." This is my attempt to keep things casual. "No, I know."

"I used to try to carry that load too. I really did. I realized I didn't have to. Blake showed me someone else was there to do that. He's been there all along."

SHERYL AND BLAKE offer to let me to spend the night, but yeah right. No thanks. There are a lot of strange things I might consider doing on this road trip, but shacking up with the wonder twins there—no way. I might be motivated a bit too much for my liking, not to mention being loved right out their front door.

The Starbucks conversation never gets too deep because I don't allow it to. We do talk about music and the state of the industry, and Sheryl shares a few new albums she likes. Then, a bit to my horror, she buys me a couple of albums they sell at the counter. It's still strange for me to see how music is made and packaged and sold these days. I joke with Sheryl that I asked for a Venti album and she just gives me a strange look. I'm content to know that not all of my humor translates.

The first album is one of those Adele wannabes who have suddenly sprouted up on the scene. I'm suspicious and skeptical, but then it only takes two songs until I'm sold. You can't overproduce passion and you can't fake something from the soul. This young lady is heartbroken and singing from a place very few of us can get to in life.

It gives me goose bumps.

Sheryl told me I'd love it and said she already had the album.

I guess she still knows me after all.

Some melodies just stick. Some music just soothes. Sometimes, in some miraculous way, a sweet soft balm of sound covers your skin. It works. It's relief.

Just like some souls coming across your path.

It's funny to know Sheryl wanted me to hear this. She has different tastes from me but I'm allowed to see the world through her eyes. To understand it through a different set of ears.

Yet love is love, right? Upbeat or downbeat or soft and smooth or loud and rough.

I'm driving, but I'm not sure where I'm driving to. I'd like to think Casey's somewhere waiting for me. Waiting to hear from me.

You had your chances.

But am I allowed another chance?

This singer is quite eccentric. She purrs. Then she starts to howl. She's screaming and I'm wondering what in the world she's singing about. It's a bit hypnotic and funky and it makes me start speeding.

I want this sort of passion. I want this sort of feeling. To rush and to run and knock down the door and to not let her let me go. I want to parade in front of her house. I want to pound down her front door. I want to strum a song and sing along and tell her I'm here and I finally belong.

These rambling thoughts make me think I might have a chance at writing some lyrics. Every time I think of Casey, the lyrics are there right on the tip of my tongue. But I try to write them down and they evaporate.

The muse is always there, like the sun, but by the time I try to capture it, it has already set in the distant sky.

Casey Writes Her Future

I REALIZE MID-MORNING THAT I spent so much time living near the historic and picturesque city of Savannah, Georgia, yet I never really spent much time soaking it in. It seems like I've spent more time in Hilton Head Island, in South Carolina, which is less than an hour away. This is one of the first times I've ever simply wandered the streets looking at the landmarks and the monuments, the historic homes with names and details posted by each one. I find myself lost for a moment, stuck back in the Civil War era, the rising sun and humidity making me sweat in my sundress.

Burke and I always spoke of getting away and staying downtown, but we always ended up going to other far-off places instead. Aruba and Mexico. Savannah was so close we could always go there, yet we seldom spent much time there besides having a meal or doing some shopping.

I'm meeting Burke for lunch and still am not quite sure what to do about the whole will thing. I put it out of my mind last night, even though I couldn't sleep. I kept thinking of how fast the past decade had gone by and how little I seemed to have traveled. Not in terms of traveling around the world, but traveling in the wonderful journey of life. I still lived in the town I grew up in, still saw my family all the time, still attended the same church, still found myself feeling like I was twenty-one and waiting to take on the world.

Before lunch, as I'm walking near the Savannah River along River Street, where all the shops and the restaurants and tourists seem to be, I discover a sign pointing to a bookstore. I wander down a street and come across a narrow shop in an old brick building called Back River Books. The door is open, so I step inside and hear the purring of a fan blowing on a shelf next to the entryway.

It smells musty in here, like a real bookstore should. The walls are lined with shelves full of books, organized in some way I can't really figure out. There is a narrow aisle that goes into the store, then opens up once you're past the checkout counter. I don't see anybody in here, so I simply start glancing at the variety of hardcover books.

An older woman greets me with a sweet Southern accent and

asks if I'm looking for anything in particular. I say I'm not and then compliment her on the bookstore. Soon I'm in the back, among even more narrow aisles and shelves reaching to the ceiling, holding row after row of books. Some are brand-new and some appear used. They're grouped by category. History, fiction, photography.

I settle in at a couple of rows of poetry. Some habits never die. It takes me about ten seconds before I see the book. I take it out and see that it's used but still in good shape.

Somewhere in the course of going to college and deciding to get "serious" with my life and falling for Burke, my childhood dreams and ambitions got put on a shelf. Much like this book. I hear the spine groan as if it's a child yawning after being awoken from a long slumber.

I used to have this edition of this book.

I hold *Love Songs* by Sara Teasdale. I think she was one of my favorite female poets, and her life fascinated me, including her tragic suicide. For a few moments, I look through the pages and remember familiar phrases and titles.

It's been so long.

Like someone dusting off the keys of a piano or cracking the knuckles on fingers that are finally ready to type again. Sometimes when you put something on a shelf, whether it's a dream or a love or a habit, the shadows and the dust can build up and eventually smother it.

I let out a sigh. I never knew what I really wanted to do with my love of writing and poetry. I just knew I wanted to do something more than teach it.

I see the poem that was one of my favorites.

"The Kiss."

The first time I read it was in college. I remember thinking of Daniel then, just like I do now. I still have the key lines memorized:

> *His kiss was not so wonderful*
> *As all the dreams I had.*

Dreams are good things, beautiful things. They don't belong on a shelf in the back but on a display in the front window. They deserve to be seen, even if you can't afford them and can only walk past them. They need to be noticed and appreciated and never, ever forgotten.

I bring the book up to the front register. I need a few dreams to come back into my life. Today I'm going to buy one, and it only costs a couple of dollars.

WE'RE ON THE balcony of a well-known seafood restaurant that Burke and I have eaten at several times before. He ordered us some crab cakes and fried pickles and I'm already starting to feel full. Full and very unhealthy. A couple of men who Burke knew from somewhere sat down at the end of the balcony, so he excused himself for a moment to say hello. I sip my iced tea and take note of the fact that Burke ordered the same. Usually he wouldn't be able to refrain from having a cocktail or two at lunch.

A part of me wonders again what I'm doing here. I know the technical answer, but life isn't lived in technical terms.

Sometimes the hardest person to be honest with is yourself. You get used to hearing the lies you tell others, the ways you fake being happy and being hopeful and being okay with life. You fake it so much that you begin to believe that life and that attitude.

A part of me knows I came back to see Burke because a part of me still wants to be with him. Perhaps it's the messed-up and highly dysfunctional part, but it's a part nonetheless. I wonder whether it's better to be discontented with someone or to be on your own. Lately, I've really wondered that a lot, believing the latter is tougher. Even if the love and passion aren't there, someone is still there to occasionally listen to you or look your way or feel a little longing in their heart.

You're sounding like a seventy-five-year-old widow.

It's not that I haven't had any opportunities since the divorce was final. There have been men who have asked me out, and there have been a few times I actually said yes.

I find myself thinking back to the last date I went on several months ago, the one who told me maybe I should be a little more careful about who I said yes to. It wasn't like this guy Karl was a creepo into weird things. He was a perfectly nice guy I met at my church through a friend of a friend. I wasn't about to start attending a Sunday-school class for divorcees—I just couldn't do that. I didn't want to be a part of a group of people who were in their mid-thirties and weren't married.

This guy was someone I'd spoken with a few times casually, and he seemed normal. He asked me out for dinner, and I accepted.

I didn't realize accepting meant going to a family barbeque. A family barbeque where I felt like I was meeting them in preparation for the wedding. At one point in the evening, I'd pulled Karl aside and asked him what was going on. He was oblivious, asking me if I was okay and whether or not I liked the ribs and if I had spoken to Grandma S. I told him the ribs were fine and Grandma S was fine and *why in the world didn't you tell me I was meeting your whole entire family?* Karl just laughed and didn't understand why I was so freaked out.

Turns out, as my friends eventually told me, Karl thought I overreacted just a bit. I thought that was funny, considering how he overdated just a bit as well. Needless to say, we didn't go out again. I always wondered what in the world a second date with Karl would look like anyway.

I haven't been hiding from the world these past four years. Some of the friends Burke and I had have stayed in touch even since I moved back to Asheville. All of my sisters are still in the area, along with Mom and Dad. In some ways I still feel young, like I'm twenty-five and fresh out of school. Yet the mirror and my weary soul remind me I'm just making that up. I'm tired. I'm tired and have been for a long time.

"Sorry about that," Burke says as he sits down. "Those guys worked with my father. They were just sharing their condolences."

I nod and smile.

"You haven't finished these yet?" he asks about the fried pickles.

"I think if I lived here I'd be twice as big."

He dips the breaded pickle into the ranch dressing. I know Burke doesn't eat like this either, not considering his lean frame. He's always been able to eat whatever he wants, but he's not twenty-one anymore either.

"So have you decided it's okay to have a summer home in Savannah?"

I shake my head. "I can't."

"You can't move?"

"I can't accept it. There's just no way."

The energy on his face from talking with the men at the end of the balcony suddenly disappears. He nods and takes a sip of his sweet tea.

"Burke—did you really think I'd be fine with that?"

"I don't know."

"It's taken me quite a while to just deal with life after moving back to Asheville."

"After moving back to Asheville" sounds a lot kinder than "after you bailed on me" or "after you decided to go ahead with the divorce."

"I can tell you how much I've changed, but there's no way you'll believe me."

"Nope," I say.

"That's why I just want—why I need some time."

I think of familiar responses, but I hold my tongue. I wipe a bead of sweat off my temple and then glance out at the river.

"How long are you going to be around?" he says.

"As long as I need to be. I assume I have to sign some papers."

I see his glance shift as if I said something important. Then I understand.

Yeah, I already signed some papers. Some really important papers that I signed with a chunk of my bleeding heart.

"Can I just ask you one thing? And be honest?"

I nod. "I've always been honest with you."

"Have you seen Daniel? Is he back in your life?"

This is surprising. "Why would you ask that?"

"I'm not an idiot. I know—I knew he was always interested in you. Even after we married."

This is a subject that's never directly come up. Indirectly at times. But not stated as simply as this.

"I guess he eventually got smart and decided to stop chasing me after all these years," I say, trying to be casual and witty about it.

I know the truth, though, and it's not as flippant as that statement.

Burke leans over and takes my hand. "Yeah, well I got smart and decided I should've been chasing you all along. Biggest mistake of my life."

I smile and then gently take back my hand. It's dangerous when Burke talks like that. It's statements like this that made me fall for him in the first place.

Here we stand and here we fall
A boy who wants to be a man
A little girl standing so tall
The shadows of our souls
Follow us on this floor
We dance to feel whole
Knowing there's gotta be more.
—Sparkland & Winter, "More"

WEDDING BELLS

(2002)

Your Song

THE CHÂTEAU-STYLED MANSION resembled a castle, and it stood in the center of a sprawling estate tucked in the middle of the rolling hills around Asheville. Like so many things in his life, Daniel had seen and heard of and even been at the Biltmore House, but he'd never really paid much attention to it. Now the 250-room home with its gardens and winery and village overwhelmed him. And he was indeed a bit breathless, but it was more because of this day than because of the location.

He had been outside and seen the rows of chairs split down the middle with a white runner. There was an immaculate floral wedding arch at the front. Only a few of the guests had arrived, so there was still time.

It took a few minutes and a few questions to find the right room. It turned out they were at the nearby inn on the estate where everybody attached to the wedding would be staying.

So far, he hadn't seen anybody he recognized. As he got close to the door the woman at the desk had pointed out, Daniel heard voices from down the hallway. He sprinted and saw the door was already open a bit, so he swung it all the way open and saw Ashley standing there, her mouth wide, the burgundy bridesmaid's gown wrapped around her tiny waist. He put his finger to his mouth, even though he knew there was no way Casey's youngest sister would keep quiet.

"You're not supposed to be here!" the tallest and loudest version of the Sparkland sisters shouted.

"Is she . . . ?" He pointed to the back of the room, a large room full of bouquets and bags and makeup and mirrors.

"What are you doing?" Ashley said.

"I need to talk with her."

Just then, the bride walked out in a dizzying, dazzling glow of white. Daniel looked at her and knew there was no way he could fully take in her beauty. He had imagined what she would look like on this momentous day, but no image he created in his mind competed with the stunning bride in front of him.

"Daniel—"

"Please, can we have just a minute?" he said to Ashley, who

looked as confused as Casey, but she nodded and walked out the door.

Daniel locked it and then stepped toward Casey. Her long hair was up and fell to one side. Bare shoulders looked too smooth to kiss. He'd never seen her with so much makeup on, yet it didn't hide the natural beauty he had fallen in love with. Those eyes, those freckles, those round cheeks were still the same. Elegant, refined, lovely.

"You look—"

"What are you doing here?"

"Stunning."

"Daniel—you have to leave."

"Why?"

She let out an exasperated chuckle. "I didn't even—what are you doing here? This is bad luck."

"What? To see the bride before the ceremony?"

"Yes!"

He gave her a nod, then found her hand and picked it up and gave her a kiss. He didn't want to chance kissing her cheek. His favorite Springsteen shirt and his loose jeans were a bit dirty from the trip.

"I think that usually applies to the groom."

"And ex-boyfriends."

Daniel smiled. "I had to come."

"Stop it. Just please—stop. Don't."

"Don't what?"

She turned and began walking away, her dress moving like a massive ship on the water.

"Casey, please."

"Not now. Not today. I can't do this. I'm not changing my mind."

He walked up to her as she stared out a window onto the grass below. More well-dressed people were outside, taking in the beauty of the Biltmore Estate and the crystal-clear summer day.

"So I see you decided to go with a small, understated wedding, huh?"

She looked at him, tears in her eyes.

"No, no—don't cry, not now." He found a box of tissues and gave it to her. "I didn't come to change your mind."

"Then why are you here?"

"I came to tell you some news. And to give you a present."

"No. Please—I don't want Burke knowing you're here."

"Burke, huh? I imagine he's a poor kid from the other side of the tracks, right?"

The look she gave him wasn't flattering.

"Just—please. Five minutes."

"I don't have five minutes."

"Please—just sit for a moment. That chair in front of the mirror looks comfortable."

Casey sat down on the small loveseat centered in the room. He took a small chair and sat on it.

"You are beyond beautiful, you know that?"

She finally seemed to show him a small part of her old self when a tiny crack of a smile came on her lips. "You only say that when I dress up."

"Good one. But untrue. And you know it."

"Why are you here?"

"Because of our song. The one we wrote in college. At Hilton Head. Remember?"

"No, I don't have the faintest idea what you're talking about."

He wondered if she was joking and was about to ask when a knocking sounded on the door.

"Honey, are you doin' okay?"

Daniel knew it was Casey's mother. He made a face and Casey just shook her head and told him to be quiet.

"I'm fine, Mom. Just a minute, okay?"

"You sure?"

"Yeah, I'm fine.

"I bet your sister told her," Daniel said in a whisper.

"I don't think so," Casey said. "If she had, my mother would have already called the police. Or would be trying to break down that door herself."

"Ah, the love."

"Daniel, you can't be here."

"I sold it. Or we sold it. Our song. 'My Holiday.' Well, almost. There's a new guy on the scene working on a country album and his management liked our song."

"Are you serious?"

"Yeah. His name is Jimmy Wayne. The next big thing in Nashville. He's gonna record our song."

Casey let out a slight scream. "Are you kidding me?"

"No."

"Stop it. You're lying."

"The only thing is—it's our song. There's some paperwork for you to sign."

"Now?"

Daniel laughed. "No. Later. There's lots of paperwork and numbers and rights and all that."

"That song is yours. I told you."

"I know you did. But still—half of it is yours, even if I owe the whole song to you."

"The melody was all yours, Daniel."

"You inspired every note and every chord. And pretty much all the lyrics are from you."

Her enthusiasm faded a bit with that comment.

"I'm sorry," he said. "Look, I just had to tell you this. I just found out the other day, and I didn't even know you were getting married."

"I told you I was engaged last time you called."

"I know. That was like a year ago, right? And I just—a part of me always thought—I don't know."

"I'm proud of you," she said.

"Of us, Casey. Of us."

"Yeah."

The knocking sounded again. "Case? Please open this door."

Casey stood up and went to the door, opening it and whispering a few things before shutting it again.

"I need to finish getting ready. You know—for my *wedding*."

"Yeah. Just—here. I have something else for you."

He took the CD from his jacket pocket. "I wrote this. For you. In thanks."

"Another song?"

"Yeah. Except. It's a wedding gift. My gift is my song, and this one's for you."

A smile filled her face. "Oh, really?"

"Ever hear that one before?"

"Sounds like an Elton John song you stole," Casey said.

Daniel laughed. "Hey—good job. Your musical tastes are expanding."

"I learned a few things while we were together."

"Look—I knew there was really nothing I could give you for your wedding, so I gave you the only thing I could. I really hope you'll be happy, Casey. I really do."

"Thank you."

He nodded, looking at her again like he was taking one last glance at some immaculate image he'd forever be haunted by the rest of his life. "You know—I only wrote the music, because that's the thing I'm good at. If things don't work out with your guy—I mean . . . if he turns out to be a real tool—then maybe one day you can let me know. Maybe we can fill in the blanks and write the story for this song."

She looked like she could have said anything, like she wanted to say so many things, yet Casey gave him a nod and just said, "Thank you for coming today."

They looked at each other with a fond, familiar glance that

meant more than anything else either of them could have said.

"So," Daniel said, a grin on his face. "I have to ask."

"No you don't."

"Are you gonna kiss me or not?"

Casey shook her head and smiled, taking his arm and guiding him back out of the room. "No, Mr. Winter."

"Just a little farewell kiss."

"I recall we already had that, you know, when we said *good-bye*."

"How about a kiss for old time's sake?"

She opened the door and proceeded to start nudging him out. "You never change, you know?"

"Nope. Never."

"Good-bye."

She began to shut the door. Daniel stayed there for a moment, the smile still on his face, the glow still in his heart. Then he heard voices coming down the hallway. He looked the other way, then sprinted away from the coming crowd.

A part of him believed he wasn't going to see Casey. He couldn't believe he had not only seen her but spoken with her and given her his song.

He was happy for himself and happy for her.

Daniel wanted Casey Sparkland to be happy. Her smile confirmed that she was.

Tell Me I'm Crazy

IT TOOK ALMOST three weeks to finally listen to that CD. A part of Casey knew she should have thrown it away, but she was curious. Curious and concerned. She wondered if there was something more on the CD than a song. Perhaps a message or a warning or something that Casey needed to hear.

It was summer and their ten-day honeymoon to Hawaii was over and Burke had finally gone back to work. She had another few weeks off before her school year started. She still didn't feel fully moved into the new house they had bought, but she was getting there. Like a new pair of jeans, this home and this life took a little time getting comfortable with.

Then there was Daniel's gift to think about. It felt like something open-ended, something that needed taking care of. He had said good-bye and given her his present. Now it was up to her to open it up and deal with it.

He's been out of my life for four years.

Yet while this was true, it really wasn't true.

They had said their good-byes and gone their own ways. Daniel had gone to New York for a year, which had only proven he wasn't the sort of frontman for a band that he wanted to be. It seemed tough, from the few times she heard from him. He called a couple times out of the blue, just to say hi and to see how she was doing. There were no midnight calls in the middle of thunderstorms where he professed his undying love to her. No heart-felt tear-stained poems sent to her.

A few times they had run into each other, once even grabbing a quick bite to eat together. Their chemistry and connection were still there. But by then Casey had Burke in her life, and Daniel had his music.

He had once written her an e-mail saying he was living back at home. Not long after that came news that his father had started to become ill. It took her a couple of conversations with Daniel to discover that was why he had moved back home, and maybe why some of those musical dreams had been put on hold.

Her relationship with Burke had been mentioned in their passing conversations. She never bothered to tell Burke about Daniel. He wouldn't have been worried even if she had. The world according to Burke meant not worrying about other guys, especially those who had dropped out of college to pursue a music career that was going nowhere. Burke would have just laughed and forgotten about Daniel, and Casey didn't want that part of her life being so easily overlooked.

Somehow, in some weird way, this CD felt like part of Daniel and that life. Maybe it was, in fact, just a simple song. But she knew no song was simple to Daniel. She could still remember him calling her a couple of years earlier talking about this new band he'd discovered and the straightforward melodies they had.

"This group is called Coldplay and they're a bit slow and moody but it's really cool, like something I could see myself singing or writing."

Casey wondered if there was someone else Daniel could confide things like that to, but so far she hadn't seen signs of anybody in his life. The CD once again seemed to confirm that Daniel hadn't let her go so easily.

The silence felt like a thick blanket covering her. She held the CD like a live grenade that needed to be tossed.

Don't do this to yourself.

She finally told herself she was strong enough to listen to a song. If she couldn't do that, then heaven forbid Daniel come knocking on her front door. She slipped the disc into Burke's expensive stereo and saw there was only one track. One song.

Just a song and nothing else.

She pressed Play and listened to the four-minute-track. It was a soft guitar melody.

A minute in, she began to cry.

I'm being stupid, totally stupid.

The song sounded so simple and so ordinary and so . . .

Haunting.

She could imagine all the unwritten lyrics that should've accompanied this melody. All the unspoken words that would have sounded so fitting and so good.

Casey wiped the tears and scolded herself for being so emotional. It was just a song from a guy she used to like. That's all.

But of course it's not all, and you know it.

The song eventually drifted off like the vapor caused by a jet plane high in the sky. It left a streak across her heart and nobody else might see it, but Casey could see it very clearly.

She took the CD out and thought about throwing it away. But instead, she marked it "My Song" and then put it in one of her favorite CD cases so she wouldn't forget it.

Daniel's song rested in the case for Shelby Lynne's *Temptation*.

In a weird way, that seemed perfect. A bit too perfect.

I can see the sunset
But can never find the sunrise
I can feel your heart rest
Whenever I look you in the eyes
Two souls without a care
Two smiles without a frown
We're travelers going nowhere
Going nowhere but down.
—Sparkland & Winter, "More"

PRESENT DAY

Daniel Drives and Calls

WHAT MAKES A love song work? What makes a sad song truly tragic instead of sappy? What makes it speak to a whole host of people out there, an entire generation?

I read the text from my manager that confirms our meeting in a few days. I curse and wonder what I'm going to play for him. I have a few songs but nothing really special. Nothing any more special than the demo songs I sent him a long time ago.

I feel like I'm trying to cram for an exam that I'll be taking very soon. I'm cramming and still don't have the faintest clue how I'll do on the test. Right now, I feel I'd fail.

The last three albums I listened to—let's see . . . *The Best of Eric*

Clapton. Awesome record, awesome vibe, awesome everything. His masterpiece "Wonderful Tonight" is maybe one of the sexiest songs out there. This is the song to dance to on your wedding night, the one that makes the crowd disappear and makes your bride blush because she knows what you're thinking.

Listening to it made me think of Casey. Because of course, I've got this bad habit of thinking of a girl I haven't been with forever who somehow stole my heart and soul and then disappeared.

I switch things up and put some Black Keys in. This suddenly makes the car go a little faster and my heart race a little quicker and I suddenly feel myself again. The old Daniel Winter, the guy pre-*Donut* years. The guy who still dated and still longed for ladies and still felt like there was a promise of leaving some legacy behind. The guy behind the two hit singles. The guy with a cool vibe. The guy with some promise.

I can imagine someone I would never be, and this is the beauty of music. The music filling your car could change your course. At least temporarily.

I change pace and put on Taylor Swift's latest release, a peppy and fun album that continued to show her range of talents. My dream song would be sung by Taylor Swift. Okay, it would be Bruce, but there would almost be no chance of that ever happening. At least my last few songs were country hits, so it was more likely (though still one in a billion) that the young starlet might sing some song of mine.

It's easy to think that once an artist has massive success, they're some kind of sellout or some part of a slick machine. The truth is

there's always something brilliant and beautiful about the top artists of all time. When they break out and hit it big, the world
watches and waits. To stay on top is difficult. To stay brilliant and
beautiful is crazy hard.

I like listening to the greatest of the greats. Michael Jackson,
for instance. Before the craziness that became his life, there was
the undeniable talent. *Thriller* is a spectacular album. Period.
Doesn't matter what genre you care for or what kind of vibe you're
going for. Try not to move when listening to "Wanna Be Startin'
Somethin'."

Perhaps those young stars burning bright these days, like Taylor Swift and so many others, have learned from the legacy of pop
stars. All I know is that while a part of me is sad that I never had
any sort of career performing and making music, I'm glad to have
never had the spotlight on me. I would have hated it. I love making songs in my little solitary life and seeing what becomes of
them. It's easier that way. It's always easier performing in the shadows rather than standing onstage under the bright lights.

The melodies fill my soul and I want to find a place where I
can make a few of mine with my guitar. Yet I'm still hours away
from Chicago, where I'll be stopping by and seeing my brother.
So I do what I've done many times before, humming the tunes
into my iPhone to record pieces of them while continuing to hope
and believe.

To hope and believe in something brilliant and beautiful.

★ ★ ★

IT'S A WEIRD thing to know you have everything you own in the back of your two-door and slightly beat-up Mazda Miata. It's not like I ever intended to become someone like this, some loner guy who decides to get rid of his belongings and head into the wild. But I also never wanted to have some mansion on some estate with a fleet of vehicles and possessions and responsibilities hanging around my neck like a noose. I've always wanted to be free. But the sound of my engine and the light on the dashboard makes it clear that I'm not free, just like everybody else. We're still all bound by something. We're still all prisoners here, no matter how far we might go or what we might do.

I make it to a small town named Claresboro, Nebraska. It's the middle of the day and the trucking station doesn't look too crowded. I know my car needs some more coolant and maybe it needs a break.

It needs a new owner who will take care of it instead of someone who barely remembers to check the oil.

Inside, I ask a guy who looks like an off-duty Santa Claus if someone can take a look at the engine. He hollers for a Charlie, and I spend the next half hour watching a lanky guy named Charlie staring at my engine and fiddling around with it. He then suggests I put some coolant in the engine and let it rest for a while.

The guy's a genius.

To kill some time, I decide to eat. I don't take good care of myself, to be honest. Hating your job can make you forget life's essentials. Getting canned from a job you hate can make you forget almost anything. Then seeing your ex-fiancée and hearing her tell you the breakup was the best thing that ever could have happened to her can make you a little angsty. I get a burger and some fries and sit in a booth. I look out at the truckers and the travelers fueling up on their journey toward somewhere.

That's your problem—you don't know where you're headed and never have.

I think I did. Once. When I dropped out of college and tried to make the band work. We were called Corner of the Page. What kind of name was that? That sure didn't sound like a band waiting to break out. But I assumed focusing on the band and living in New York and taking a break from Casey (just a break, not the permanent separation it ended up being) would all be good decisions in the long run. I believed things would fall into place as long as the songs were good enough and as long as we could find some fans who loved them. But the songs never came. Casey went away. The fans were a no-show before the concert tickets ever got printed.

I'm thirty-five and I have a collection of songs about doughnuts.

There are the songs you've written with Casey.

Sparkland & Winter gems. Like the fingers on my hands, I could number each one.

"You waiting for someone, sweetheart?"

The voice takes me by surprise, just like the dark eyes staring down at me. The woman standing by my table is tall and attractive, with a bit of an edge. With a bit of a history. Yet, strangely, I don't think she's out of place in the middle of this truck stop.

"Waiting on my car to cool down," I tell her.

She slides in across from me without shifting her gaze an inch. "And what about you? Are you waiting to cool down too?"

For some reason I burst out laughing. I don't mean to laugh at her. I'm not trying to laugh at her or her line or whatever she's trying to do here. It's just—it's so corny and I'm so tired.

"I think I've permanently cooled down. My career. My prospects. My life."

The woman looks at me and knows I'm not interested in anything other than polite conversation. From far away she'd look ten years younger, but the wrinkles etched around her eyes and lips tell another story. She smiles but this time in a more genuine, friendly way.

"Where are you headed?"

"Chicago. Then back down South. I'm from North Carolina."

"That is a long ways from here."

I nod. "Yeah. I've been gone for some time."

"I used to live in Florida."

"Serious?"

The woman nods. It's strange when the softest thing about a woman is the shirt she's wearing. Everything else about her looks hard, as if it were cut with a jagged knife.

"How'd you end up here?"

"It's a sad story."

"It's the stuff of country songs," I say, quoting a lyric I had just heard from a U2 song not long ago. "Could make you a fortune."

"My fortune passed me by on I-80 going ninety miles an hour."

I give her a polite smile. Both of us have our sad stories to tell.

Perhaps other men might choose to ignore those sad country songs and instead put on a new rocking track. A track that blocks out the rest of the noisy world and focuses on the woman across from him.

But I'm not other men and I've never been other men.

"I'm Daniel," I say, holding out my hand in a formal and polite manner.

She takes it, amused at the formality. "I'm Mya."

For a moment, I'm not sure what to say. I'm not completely oblivious to what's happening here. But anything I think of saying, like "Live around here?" sounds like bad lines. She seems to understand the silence and she reaches over to grab a fry. She eats it and then gives me a nod.

"I hope you find what you're looking for," she tells me.

"What if I don't know exactly what I'm looking for just yet?"

"I think you know. The question is whether or not *she* knows as well."

"That obvious?"

She nods, smiles, then slides back out of the booth.

IT'S ALWAYS INTERESTING how two people can come together in a random way and connect. Sure, at a truck stop where a lady named Mya is asking me what my plans are—well, perhaps there's a very definitive reason we're getting together at this particular time. Two souls connecting in any way.

What if Casey had never caught my attention that first day of senior year?

I think she would've caught my attention another day in another way.

What if she had acted more friendly and hadn't made me so angry? Would I have been that interested that quickly?

Like a cross-country trip without a map, every relationship has so many twists and turns, one road leading to a hundred others.

It's late afternoon and I'm almost in Chicago and I decide to do something very stupid.

I call Casey's mother's house. She's still living on the same road in the same house with the same phone number. I still refer to Krista Sparkland as Mrs. Sparkland and always will. She's always had that proper sense about her. I'm just hoping—*hoping*—that she will tell me the truth about where Casey might be.

Or maybe Casey will actually answer the phone.

"Hello?"

It's the voice of the woman who has hated me from day one.

Maybe she's changed.

"Mrs. Sparkland?"

"Burke? Is that you?"

Stick the knife right in my gut.

"Uh, no. This is Daniel."

"Daniel." She says the word as if it's an abomination. "What do you want?"

"Is Casey there?"

"Casey hasn't been here for a long time."

It doesn't quite sound like Mrs. Sparkland has had a change of heart with good ol' Daniel Winter.

"Would you know where she is?"

"Why are you calling, Daniel?"

"Because I want to get in touch with Casey."

"Haven't you learned? How much time will have to pass before you learn?"

I really detest this woman. Part of me wonders if Casey and I would be together if it wasn't for her.

"Some people are a bit more stubborn I guess," I tell her.

"Casey is with Burke right now. His father passed and she decided to go down there and tend to him. I told her now would be a good time to stop with her foolishness and reunite with Burke. They've always belonged together."

I want to ask if she's making this up but I can tell she's not.

"So when are you going to go ask Casey's father about getting back together?"

"Dear boy," the Carolina accent began. "If you think that's gonna hurt my feelings, you don't know me."

"No. I just wanted to say something as ludicrous as the stuff coming out of your mouth."

Mrs. Sparkland used a colorful word to describe me, then her words grew slower and softer. "Now, you listen to me, you little piece of trash. When are you gonna learn to leave Casey alone? Huh? She's never been a part of your life and never will be and that's that."

Suddenly I'm guessing my wonderful little note never got to Casey.

I'm about to say something else when the line goes dead.

I let out a sigh and then think of Casey and Burke.

Everything that's happened seems to scream at me to leave Casey alone and move on with my life. But everything inside of me says there's still a chance.

Just like that song I've been looking for.

I'm not letting go. Not yet. Not now. Not after all this time I've kept believing.

That's the moment I decide I'm going to drive to Casey and find her and sing her one last song, whatever it might be.

If it's the last song I ever write then so be it. I'll go out with a bang.

Casey Wonders by the Fountain

*I*T FEELS GOOD to be back outside under the afternoon sun. We'd spent two hours in an office in downtown Savannah with one of Burke's lawyers (it's news to me that he has several) going over the details of my disclaimer of the will. A document was written up, notarized, signed by me, and witnessed by this lawyer. At some point they might have to file this in court as part of the probate estate. I was just glad they didn't need me to have a lawyer present and that there wasn't any dramatic family stuff to deal with. As Burke told me, he'd deal with his sister, Bridgett. I wouldn't have to worry about her.

A huge sense of relief followed me back out into the blanket of humidity. Burke asks me if I feel good about my decision and I tell him I do.

"This still doesn't mean you have to leave," Burke says.

"I'm still staying in Hilton Head a few more days."

Burke stops me and looks down at me on the city sidewalk. "No, I mean leave me. Leave us."

"Burke, please—"

He's about to say something when his phone rings. He glances at me and knows what this means. This was one of the many areas of frustration when it came to us. He never left his job behind. Yet in this case, the distraction is a good one. He waits for me to say something and I simply nod. When he sees who's calling, he tells me he'll be right back.

We're close to Forsyth Park, so I begin to walk down one of the paths toward the large fountain. I recall at one point walking here with Burke, but all I can remember about that is arguing with him about something. It takes me a few moments to reach the fountain. I walk underneath ancient trees with limbs leisurely hovering over the path like some kind of ornate dome. The centerpiece itself is an impressive two-tiered, cast-iron fountain that could have been stolen from somewhere in Greece. At the top of the fountain is a woman in a robe holding a rod.

I notice a woman pushing a baby stroller. She looks to be someone my age, maybe a little younger, maybe older. The woman looks tired but she also looks happy.

Maybe "happy" isn't the right word for it.

Fulfilled, maybe. Content.

I watch her for a few moments and feel that familiar tug that's come the last few years. It used to come with Burke, but I would hide it. Sometimes I would take it and lock it away in a silent and dark place. That's one reason I probably stayed longer than I should have with Burke. The promise that he would change, that our life would change, that this woman walking in the park could one day be me.

"Hey," Burke calls from behind me. "You disappeared."

"Just walking."

He nods, then glances at the woman I'd been staring at. Or gawking might be the appropriate word.

"Sorry about that," he says.

"Oh, it's fine."

We stand there and stare at each other and suddenly it's awkward. I've shared a lot of moments with this man—passionate ones, heated ones, sorrow-filled ones—but very few like this. Where we're both at a loss for what to say or do.

"Want to walk with me?" I ask him.

"Okay."

It takes a few moments before he puts my thoughts and feelings into words.

"There's still time to start a family."

Everything inside of me has to hold back tears. Not because I desperately want to have this man's child, but because of that very word, "family." It used to symbolize something more until the colorful photo of our lives began to fade out and become black and white. I dreamed we'd have a family, only to awaken one day and realize it would never, *ever* happen.

He knew exactly what I was thinking back there at the fountain.

"Burke—"

"Just hear me out, okay? You signed your papers and you're free to go and that's all fine, but just hear me out. If you didn't want to be here, you wouldn't be. Right?"

I nod, staring at the emblem on his clean and pressed polo shirt.

"We can pick up where things were left. I mean, back when you wanted me to go to counseling with you. Back when there was a chance."

"We can't just back up."

"Says who?" Burke says. "Who says we can't? I put our lives on hold and made a lot of mistakes."

"A lot."

"But I still love you. I realize—you're the only good thing I have left in this world."

You don't have me anymore, you gave that up when you wanted another life with booze and women.

"There's still time," Burke tells me. "And you gotta think about the times we're living in. These days—I don't care who you are, money's an issue. But it's not for me. And I could focus on us and we could finally try and have that family we always talked about. We don't have to live in that house in Savannah. We don't even have to live around here."

"How can you suddenly bring all of this up? Out of the blue?" I see streaks of sunlight coming through the towering oak trees.

"I think about you every day. This isn't out of the blue for me.

My father's passing and his will brought you back into my life. You said yourself there's nobody else, and you're here with me now."

"I had to come down."

"I know you believe in second chances and forgiveness."

I can only shake my head. "You already had your second and third and fourth chances."

"Do you like being alone?"

I look up at the square face of the man I both loved and hated and I can't help the curse coming from my mouth. "The only reason I'm alone is because of the poor choice I made when you decided to chase after me."

"I'm not trying to hurt you."

"No, 'cause you already did that, years ago."

"I want to spend the rest of my life making up for that."

"No."

Burke holds my arm and stops me from walking. Not in a forceful way, but with a gentle touch. "I want to give you the life you had back. And I want to add to that life. I know how much you'd love a little boy or a girl. Casey, I know. It used to freak me out thinking about it. Now I can't stop thinking about it."

"A part of me can't stand being around you."

"I'm asking you—I'm begging you in a totally sober manner to give us a chance. It doesn't have to be conventional, but what is conventional these days? A lot of people don't even believe in marriage. I'm not asking this because I want that photo at Christmastime. I don't like being alone. I don't like knowing if I die I'll have nobody."

"That's the choice you made."

"Yes, I know, and once again, I'll tell you I'm sorry. I was wrong. But I'm here and I'm asking that you let me come back in your life. I can change and will change. For you."

"Maybe you should change for yourself."

Burke curses and laughs as he gives me a big fat grin. "You're hard to win over."

"No, not really. Only once you destroy my life and break my heart into a million pieces."

"So every month I try to put those pieces back together. A little bit day by day, week by week, month by month."

The tears fall and I can't stop them. I try to wipe them away, but Burke beats me to it. He wipes them and then holds my head in his hands. I glance around us but I don't really care whose nearby. He leans over and kisses me and I kiss him back. I still love him and still hate him and still want to have a life with him and still want nothing to do with him. It's a joyful and painful sort of thing, this man in front of me.

This man I can't let go. The man I finally pull myself away from and give a big sigh to.

"You shouldn't have done that," I tell him.

"You didn't seem to mind."

He wears his grin well, like an expensive set of shades.

"I don't know what to think about all this," I say, then quickly add, "I need to be by myself."

"That's fine. I can take you back to your hotel—"

"I have a car and can drive myself. I just need some time. Some space. Okay?"

"Casey, look, I just—"

"Would you shut up and listen to me for a minute? I heard everything you said and I'm still here. You're right. You know me and you're right. I heard everything and yet I still kissed you. I just—I have a lot to think over."

"Sure, sure. Yeah, totally."

For a minute, he waits to see if I'm going to walk back to the parking lot, where we left our cars. When I don't, he nods and tells me good-bye and tells me he'll see me soon.

I find a bench and sit for a very long time in that park, thinking a lot of things over and over and over again.

All my life's been spent dreaming
All your life's been spent scheming.
—Sparkland & Winter, "Treasure" (unpublished)

Intersections

(2003–2005)

She's the One

SONGS HAVE A way of waking you up out of your wonderfully dormant life.

For Daniel, it happened the moment he opened the CD from the label and played the song. Their song, the one Casey and he had written. Sung by a soulful singer named Jimmy Wayne on his self-titled album. The song came after a series of beautiful tunes about love lost and gained and even one about something called paper angels. To hear the song they'd created gave him goose bumps. Every time Jimmy Wayne sang the words "My Holiday," Daniel felt like he was being pinched. Near the end of the song, he was in tears, because no matter how close he felt to this song, there was no way he could have captured the heart of it the way this singer did.

The next morning, after a night of little sleep, Daniel woke and realized he still loved Casey. It didn't matter that it had been a year since she got married and several years since they broke up. He had heard a host of voices in his sleep the night before.

When are you finally going to settle down?

What do you want anyway?

I can't be someone I'm not.

This isn't really going anywhere.

How can you write about love when you seem scared by it?

This last question in particular kept haunting him. It had been one of the last things Trish had said to him. Trish Anderson, his girlfriend of about four months, whom he'd met in Asheville while playing at a bar with his band. One of the last things before she called it quits, even though there hadn't really been much of a thing to quit.

After his last conversation with Trish, Daniel had gone to bed replaying the last few relationships he'd had in his mind. Every one of them paled in comparison to Casey. Every one felt like a B-side to an amazing song on an untouchable album.

That song and album are Casey.

Long-lost Casey. Long-gone Casey.

Still living in Asheville with his drunk of a father and his drunken bunch of friends, Daniel wondered if he needed to do something drastic.

Like drop out of college and break up with Casey and move to New York.

Yeah, that had been drastic, and not in a good way. He had read so many success stories about musicians making a break for something and then hitting it big. Daniel had only managed to hit the curb with his rear. His band had imploded and he'd finally realized he couldn't really sing and he also realized he couldn't really write songs. So much for the rousing success story.

He was twenty-five and thinking about a girl he would never have while trying to make songs out of an empty soul. Daniel knew what his problem was. The songs were only melodies without her soul inside of them. In the years since he'd broken up with her, Daniel tried to believe otherwise, but it was painfully true. He could capture a sound and a spirit but could never seem to match their substance with words. They would remain half finished while his dreams remained half filled. He didn't want to say Casey completed him, but his heart said otherwise. His heart always seemed to know.

Her wedding in 2002 was one of the events he had named a star to remember it by. He knew where the burning bright little spot was and he'd recall it as summer turned to fall. Once, before the end of that year, as winter threatened to arrive, Daniel ached to know how she was doing. He could no longer just pick up the phone or e-mail her. She wasn't his to contact anymore.

Yet he still tried.

He sent an e-mail to her old address, an errant toss-up like an NFL quarterback throwing a ball right before he gets sacked for a loss. He had legitimate documents to have her look over and sign, but he legitimately wanted to know how Casey was doing. To be really, truly honest, he wanted to know if she thought of him.

Casey wasn't going to admit anything like this, much less even respond.

He didn't know the protocol on e-mailing an ex. He asked how married life was and whether she'd thought about writing any more songs. He didn't get an e-mail back. A week later, he received the signed documents in the mail. No note, no hello, nothing.

The e-mail was sent sometime in November, and by the time the New Year arrived, Daniel doubted he'd ever hear from Casey again. There were things he wanted to tell her, but no words seemed sufficient. So instead of writing more words to her, he did the one thing that came naturally. He wrote musical poems. Each composition had Casey's name written all over it. Each one sounded exactly like how he felt toward her. Each song was about whatever it was he felt toward Casey, feelings he didn't exactly know how to articulate himself.

Maybe it was the memory of seeing her in the room all made up and ready to be married. Maybe it was the realization he'd let this beautiful creature go. Maybe it was the thousand things he wanted to say but couldn't that all got summed up into some beat and some blissful tune. The lyrics would remain unspoken, just like his feelings toward her.

He wanted to share with her how incredible their song sounded as sung by Jimmy Wayne. He wanted to listen to it with her and watch her discover the song herself. Of course, he wouldn't have this opportunity. Maybe she would get a copy of the CD, and maybe she would listen and like it, and maybe she'd contact him.

I can spend a whole lifetime waiting for those maybes to knock on my door.

He was already living the life of waiting for maybes to come around. One more didn't bother him. He was used to it by now.

IN APRIL OF 2003, Daniel sent Casey a short and simple e-mail.

Hey Casey.

I hope you're doing well! I'm sure married life is treating you well.

Not sure if you heard but "My Holiday" has been number one for three weeks straight. A lot of people are talking. Doors are opening. It's happening. Not exactly in the way I once imagined it would happen, but I guess that's life.

Maybe we'll have to write another song sometime. Something to think about. Half of "My Holiday" is yours and always will be.

Drop me a line if you can. Would love to hear from you. Best wishes.

Daniel

So formal and so full of it.

Maybe we'll have to write another song sometime.

Written so casually, as if it's just a random thought and not some kind of desperate hope resting on a ledge and hanging, hanging. Written without a care in the world when every ounce of him cared.

Do you want another song or do you want Casey?

It was an honest question only he could ask himself and only he could avoid.

DANIEL KNEW THAT Casey and Burke lived in Savannah, close to his relatives, but he also knew she might be coming back to Asheville to see relatives or friends or people she once wrote a top song with. He always liked to imagine the things he'd say or do if he ran into her, knowing he'd probably do none of them.

It was December 2003 when it actually happened. Daniel was leaving the mall when he noticed the strawberry blond hair and stopped for a moment. Sure enough, it was Casey.

"What are you doing here?" he asked.

Not one of those things he'd dreamed of saying.

"Shopping." Casey pointed toward the mall. "You know— that's what people do at these things."

He had laughed and then hugged her and she felt just as right as she had years ago.

"So you're visiting family?"

"Yeah. Been here for a few days. We're celebrating Christmas this weekend. We'll be celebrating in Savannah with my in-laws on Christmas weekend."

Daniel thought of making a snide remark about Casey's mother but refrained. He asked how her sisters were doing and Casey shared a little on each, then stopped herself.

"Do you want to get some coffee?" she asked him.

"Oh, man, I'd love to but I have this hot date."

"You're certainly dressed for it."

Daniel was wearing grimy and cut-up jeans and a T-shirt that said WHAT'S YOUR PROBLEM? He laughed.

"I've missed your compliments," he told her.

"I've missed your T-shirts."

"I'd love coffee. But only if I buy."

"Of course."

Every word and every sentence felt like a gift because they were so unexpected and they were from her. Daniel still knew how he felt about her and every now and then, as she talked about her teaching job or life in Savannah, he thought of telling her. Just putting it on the table. But he sometimes thought of jumping out of airplanes or flying to the moon. Thinking about something didn't mean he was going to do it.

After about the fifth time that Casey said she was doing great and that married life was wonderful, Daniel began to realize something was wrong.

But I can't ask because it's not my place and not my business.

He told her all the optimistic stuff going on in his life, all in a matter of two sentences and twenty seconds.

Soon Casey realized the time and said she needed to meet her sister Emily.

"I'm so glad to run into you," she said so casually, so *you're-just-like-all-my-other-BFFs*.

"Let me know next time you're around," he said.

Casey looked at him, a bit puzzled and even amused by the comment. "How come? So we can go out on a date?"

Daniel felt himself blush and he couldn't remember the last time that had happened. He was going to say something, anything, but Casey beat him.

"I'm sorry, that was rude."

"You still have a way with words," Daniel said.

"Only with you."

"Well, anytime you want to put them to good use—I'm always trying to come up with another number-one hit."

"I'm sure there are dozens of people out there who can help you do that."

Daniel shook his head and looked into Casey's eyes. "No, not like you."

It was the most honest thing he'd said to her all day.

IT WAS ALMOST a year later when he heard from her, close to the end of 2004. He had e-mailed her a few times to say something about their song or something he'd gotten from the label. Each time he'd never gotten anything back. Twice he'd heard that someone he knew saw her in Asheville, but she hadn't called or e-mailed or let him know she would be in town.

It was a cold Saturday in December and he was watching a

football game and was already six beers into his afternoon. Daniel knew he didn't want to be anything like his father, but this didn't stop him from drinking. He *needed* to drink in order to live with the man whose mind and liver were quickly fading away.

He answered the phone and the response was, "You're home."

"And you're calling," he said to the mysterious female voice he didn't recognize at first.

"It's Casey."

"Oh, hi, sorry. Didn't know it was you."

"Are you busy?"

"Just watching football. Riveting afternoon. Are you around?"

"Yeah. No. I mean—yes, I am. But I'm leaving."

Daniel waited for more, but she didn't say anything.

"Do you, uh, need a ride or something?"

"No, no." Casey chuckled and it was good to hear because she had sounded so serious. "It's just—I had planned on calling but I never got around to it."

"Glad you're calling."

"I don't know if that offer still stands," Casey said.

"Well, *yeah,* of course, but don't you think it might be a little inappropriate for us to go to Vegas?"

"What?"

"I'm just kidding."

She didn't seem to be in a kidding mood. Or to even get his humor.

"What offer are you talking about?" he asked.

"To write another song."

"Yes. Of course. People still keep asking me about it. 'We want another Sparkland and Winter song.'"

"Okay. I'll do it."

Daniel wasn't quite following her. "What do you mean—like, now?"

"No, no. Sometime when our schedules work out."

"I could come over and bring my guitar right now if you want."

Casey sighed. "No. I'm going to be leaving soon."

"I'm sure your mother would love to see us writing a song together."

There was just silence.

"Sorry," Daniel said. "I still get all weird whenever I talk to you. No other female on this planet has caused me to become loopy whenever I talk to them except you."

"Yes, I certainly have a way about me," Casey said.

She said this in a bittersweet way, as if she was sad.

"Is everything okay?"

"Yeah, look, I gotta go," Casey said. "I'll e-mail you and figure out a date, okay?"

"Okay. Thanks for—"

But she was gone before he could finish.

Something was wrong, and he knew it when they'd had coffee, and he knew it even more having heard her voice.

How Can I Help You Say Good-bye

"ASEY?"

The voice across the hotel lobby greeted her with a question mark more than a hello. Daniel walked toward her, looking taller and fitter than she remembered him looking. His blue eyes looked delighted to see her.

"Who's this blond lady I'm seeing?" he asked as he gave her a hug.

"Oh, yeah. I've been blond for several months now."

"I like it. It's very, uh, blond."

She shook her head. "I can see your mind spinning thinking of a joke, then pulling back."

"That obvious?"

"Have you checked in?"

He nodded his head. "Yeah, a couple hours ago. Had an early morning flight. I just got your voice mail. Your trip go well?"

"Yeah."

A tall man walked by her, and for a moment, Casey swore the guy was dressed as Elvis. Then she realized it was an Elvis look-alike.

"What—" she began to say.

"Yeah, I know. Just wait."

"Wait until what?"

"There's a celebrity look-alike convention going on this weekend in Nashville," Daniel said as if he'd been bursting to tell her that ever since he got here. "Good thing our hotel is connected to the convention center."

She saw a woman looking like Joan Rivers talking to a really bad version of Sylvester Stallone. She cringed and gave Daniel a what-are-we-doing-here look.

"They decided to invite all the crazies to one spot."

"Yeah. Great. Just what my life needs—more craziness."

Daniel chuckled but he didn't understand the depth and the gravity to her statement.

He's not going to know either, she thought.

She had just left a cyclone of a mess back in Asheville. This weekend was a chance to get away and to work with Daniel in an actual recording studio in Nashville and to forget about real life. She had no qualms about meeting Daniel now. Not after all the things she'd discovered about her husband in the past year. Yet she didn't want payback. Casey just wanted a do-over. In her marriage and love life and in the past five years.

I want to create a song and feel like I'm good at something in life since so much of it is crumbling around me.

"You look great," Daniel said.

There he goes again. First thing he's focused on is how good I look.

"Thank you."

Another voice said, *At least someone's interested in what I look like.*

If only Daniel knew.

If only he knew.

"YOU WANT A drink?" Daniel asked her as they sat on plush chairs moments later in the seating area of the sprawling Marriott luxury hotel.

"Yes. Yes I do." She said it in a way that sounded like a revelation. She hadn't eaten anything for lunch but she wasn't the slightest bit hungry. "I want something strong enough that it might make me end up streaking in the middle of the freeway a little around midnight."

Daniel gave her a bewildered and amused look. "Did the highlights seep into your brain?"

"Further than that," she told him.

Daniel went to the bar and brought back some drinks. He'd gotten two fancy cocktails and let her choose one. He didn't seem too interested in having the other one. He looked more interested in watching her.

"You're staring," she said after taking a sip.

"It's been a while."

"You saw me last year around Christmas."

"Oh, yeah, that's right. Opening presents with you on Christmas morning was an amazing experience. Wait, that's right—that never happened."

"I saw you at the outdoor mall."

"Yeah. It was freezing and we spoke for forty seconds."

"No, you're wrong," Casey said. "It was more like fifty seconds."

"You're right. How could I be so ignorant?"

"Happens to the best of us."

A trio of Madonnas walked past them in the lobby. Casey tried to contain her amusement.

"What are the odds this place would be full of celebrity look-alikes," she asked him.

"This is our first official songwriting experience, so someone I guess wanted us to have some inspiration."

"Okay, yeah, but this time we're in Nashville and have our own room to write songs in."

"You ready to come up with some songs?" she asked.

Daniel shook his head. She noticed how short and neat his hair was. It was a look he hadn't had for quite a while.

"If we don't come up with some songs, I think my manager might give up on me."

"You had a number-one single," she said. "You kept telling me how difficult those are."

"They're downright impossible. There are guys who spend their entire week cranking out songs for artists to sing."

"Have you ever thought about doing that?"

"Sometimes. I've tried too. It's just—you seem to be the missing ingredient."

"That's what all the guys say."

Daniel laughed. For a moment he paused, then he asked a polite question about how her jerk of a husband was doing.

She wanted to say something crude and crass about everything he was doing, but she refrained from saying anything other than "He's doing fine."

"Last week marked three years for you guys," Daniel said.

Casey looked up at the ceiling as she felt the room begin to turn. A pack of laughing Three Stooges walked by and just made things worse. She let out a laugh just as a shotgun burst of tears launched themselves onto her cheeks.

"Casey?"

She composed herself and kept laughing and kept trying to keep things light.

"Amazing how you remember the date better than my husband."

For the first time, Daniel reached over and took a sip of the tropical concoction with the little umbrella. "Sorry," he eventually said.

"Daniel Winter—don't you *dare* say that word around me. Not this weekend. You got that? I've heard that word uttered so many times it doesn't have a meaning anymore. It doesn't mean a thing, not when a guy says it. Not anymore."

Daniel looked like he was about to utter it again but then he remained silent.

"Aren't you glad to see me?" she joked.

"I'm always glad to see you."

He was still the earnest guy she remembered. She'd forgotten what that was like, being around a guy who said what he meant exactly when she needed something said.

"It's good to see you too," Casey said. "Maybe we'll have a little more than forty seconds this weekend."

"Fifty."

THEY WERE ON the famous Music Row of Nashville, where so many great artists had done their thing and made country-music magic. They were in Writing Room 4, a small room that had a couch and some chairs in it, along with a coffee table. In one corner was a piano. There was plenty of room to write a song. Many people had done it before them and many would do it afterward.

"Have you ever been here before?" Casey asked.

"Yeah, a couple of times."

"Really?"

"Yeah. I was brought in to try and write some songs with others."

"Who?"

Daniel smiled. "I can't really say."

"What? Are they big names?"

"Huge. And they're crazy."

"Come on, tell me."

"But they're not as crazy as my usual musical collaborator."

Casey nudged him as she sat on a chair and took out her notebook.

"That looks like the same one you had in high school," Daniel said. "I hope we come up with something better than 'The Pi Song.'"

"*That* was a great song. I still want to know who you cowrote songs with."

"I tried. Nothing ever happened. Two different people. Both needy and neurotic. One of them seriously was going through a divorce. He was a mess. He couldn't put two lines together."

"Can you?"

Daniel smiled. "You know—you have to be nice to me. We're going to be in here for a long time."

He took out his guitar and put it on the couch. The same guitar she had given him for Christmas so many years ago, the one he initially refused to accept but ultimately gave in because of Casey.

"It's nice to see that again."

"I don't go anywhere without it," Daniel said.

"You know—you should give it a name."

Daniel didn't tell her that he'd already done that.

His guitar was named May. It was the middle name of the girl he fell in love with in high school and had been chasing ever since.

THEY'D BEEN WORKING for about an hour when Daniel stopped and put down the guitar.

"What?" Casey had been singing some lyrics in a soft, drifting voice that somehow seemed to float away to another time and place.

"Do you have that written down?"

"I write everything down."

"That was—wow."

"Good?"

Daniel nodded. "Heavy, but good. I like heavy. I've been dealin' with heavy back at home with Dad. That song was written with that whole heaviness in mind."

"Yeah."

She didn't want to say more. She could fill a notebook and simply called it "Heavy Thoughts."

"You want to take a break?"

"No," Casey said. "I want to get this stuff out and then leave it behind. Leave it in this room or with you."

"How about we try and leave something with some big star."

"Fine with me," she said.

As long as it leaves me alone.

★　★　★

A SLIGHT RAIN fell as the windshield wipers waved back and forth.

"Is everything okay?" Daniel asked her at the end of their first day in the studio.

They were driving back to the hotel and the evening was dark outside.

"What do you mean? Yeah, of course. Things are fine."

"You sure?"

"Why?" She couldn't help feeling defensive.

"Well, it's just—everything you've written—all your lyrics are just really . . ."

"Just really what?"

"Sad."

"What? Sad?"

Daniel nodded.

"No they're not," Casey said.

"'I can't pull you out of the lake when you're already on dry land'? I mean—come on."

She couldn't say anything. Daniel seemed to look right through her at the tattered and torn heart she'd brought with her to Nashville.

"Look—for the songs it's fine. I mean—half of the country songs recorded are sad if you really think about them. People love sad. People need sad. I'm just worried about why you're sad."

"Aren't you Mr. Melancholy?" she asked him. "At least with your songs?"

"I can be. But not you. Not Casey Sparkland."

"That's Casey Bennett. The last name has changed. The last name has started to bleed over into everything else."

"Look, if you—"

"Daniel?"

"Yeah?"

"I'm fine. Really. I'm okay. And you don't have to worry a bit about me."

"Okay. Are you hungry? Do you want to get anything to eat?"

"I'm tired," she said, telling him the truth. At least that part of it. "I'd like to just crash for the night."

"Sure."

IT WAS MIDNIGHT when she decided to call his room.

"Are you sleeping?"

"No," a low, disoriented voice said.

"I'm sorry I woke you."

"No, it's fine. What's wrong?"

"My life. My life is what's wrong."

It took him a moment to realize what she had said. "Do you want to talk? In person?"

"No. Because I—I don't trust myself. I don't know what I'm doing here, to be honest. I think I'm running away. I know I'm running away."

"Running away from what?"

"From my husband and my life and everything I know. I

just—I don't know where to run. Except to you. Except I can't exactly do that now, can I?"

"Casey, I . . ."

"I know I'm not making any sense. I shouldn't have called."

"I wish you had called earlier."

"Earlier tonight?" she asked.

"No, like earlier, like last month or last year."

She sighed. This was wrong. Talking to him at midnight and being here in the first place and not knowing who else to turn to. She still had yet to tell any of her family about Burke.

Because I don't know what to tell them because I don't know what to do.

"Case?"

"I'm sorry I'm laying this on you."

"I want to see you."

"Seven in the morning, right?"

"I want to see you now."

"You don't want to see me now. I'm a mess."

"A beautiful mess, huh?" Daniel said. "Would love to see that."

"Why does life have to hurt so bad sometimes?"

"I don't know." For a moment there was silence over the phone. "But you're not alone, Case."

"Thanks."

There was more to say, and more that surely would be said, but for the moment it was time to tell him good night.

Here Comes the Sun

I THINK THAT'S CHUCK Norris," Daniel said to Casey while they were eating breakfast.

"A Chuck Norris look-alike?"

"No, like Chuck himself. The real Chuck Norris."

She casually glanced across the restaurant. "Why would he be here?"

Daniel shrugged, sipped his coffee, and thought of the insanity of the weekend. "Why is anybody here? I don't know. Maybe Chuck Norris doesn't have celebrity look-alikes. Maybe he's too awesome to have one."

Daniel was trying to keep the mood light after Casey's call.

He hadn't brought it up when he saw her and didn't plan on it.

"That guy almost looks better than Chuck," Daniel said.

"You're making that up."

"No, really—I'm not. I'm serious."

Casey took a bite of her fruit from the breakfast buffet, then looked up and gave a polite smile. "Sorry about the call last night."

"It was fine."

"Several months ago I found out my husband has been sleeping around. Not just with one woman but with several. Things are pretty—they're pretty intense at home."

Daniel wasn't surprised, but he still felt the sting of hearing the news. There was nothing more he wanted than to see this woman across from him happy.

"I'm sorry," he said.

"Yeah, I am too. And Burke is sorry, but that doesn't mean a whole lot. Not now."

He wanted to ask what she was going to do and when the divorce would be final and how quickly they could elope. A part of him thought of joking about that, but he decided against it.

"Now you know why everything I'm writing is so sad."

Daniel nodded and put down his fork. "How about we write a song about Chuck Norris?"

"For fun?"

"No, like total a hundred percent serious. I'm wondering if a country song has ever been written about Chuck Norris."

Casey laughed. It was good to see the tension and heaviness off her shining face. "You're crazy."

"We could have ourselves a hit."

The more he thought of it and talked about it with an unconvinced but amused Casey, the more he thought it could work. He told her names of artists who could actually do the song.

"I don't even know what the big deal with Chuck is all about."

"He was, like, in all these great action flicks in the '80s. He's got this whole mystique surrounding him. And it's just getting bigger."

"You're being serious," Casey said.

"Well, I wasn't at first but now I'm starting to think I might be."

"Don't you think your manager would flip out if we ended up giving him a Chuck Norris song?"

"Or he could think it's, like, *awesome*."

"Is he really over there?"

"I don't know. Maybe it's just an old guy with muscles and a beard."

"You're ridiculous."

The drama was gone and the sadness had disappeared. They had a whole day to spend together and Daniel felt like a teenager again.

CASEY SHOUTED AS Daniel sat watching her in silence.

The curse was unlike Casey, and unlike the day before when

they'd been working so well together. She tossed her spiral-bound notebook across the room and then stood, stretching out her neck in frustration.

"Let's just pick up at the chorus."

She gritted her teeth and looked like a stubborn toddler. "I hate this song."

"It's working."

"No, it's awful. I'm awful. I can't put together a single sentence today that makes sense."

"Maybe you're just tired."

"Yeah, tired. I'm beyond tired."

Daniel stood up and walked over to her, putting a hand on her shoulder. At his very touch, Casey flinched and jerked away as if he were some kind of monster.

"Whoa," he said.

"I'm sorry."

Casey was sorry, but still didn't look like she wanted to be consoled in any sort of way, especially physical. She moved behind a chair, as if she wanted to keep it between them.

"Want to take a break?"

"Yeah, a big break. Where I don't have to worry about things that make me want to puke. Like my husband."

He still couldn't help thinking how adorable she looked when angry. Daniel had always thought this and knew she had no idea just how beautiful she was.

"I'm sorry," he said.

"Remember when you took me away to Hilton Head? I think

about that every now and then. I've thought a lot about those days. About what might have been."

"Yeah, me too."

An intense glance lassoed around him. "I wish I could go back. I wish certain things could still be."

For a second, Daniel felt a blast of warmth go through him. He felt like he was falling, like he was breathless, like he was blushing and confused.

"I'm not making sense right now with anything I'm writing because I'm not making sense of anything in my life."

"Sense is overrated."

"Why do all the spinning storms stop when you suddenly walk into a room?"

Daniel wanted to walk over and tear away the chair and then hold her and kiss her and never let her go. Nobody had ever talked to him or made him feel the way this woman made him feel.

"That's a song," he said.

"No, it's an indictment. Maybe it's the reason I'm so messed up and my world is so messy."

"The only messiness in your life is the man you're married to."

Casey stood up and let out a groan. "I swore this wasn't going to happen."

"What?"

"This. Us. *Me.* I just—no more. No more boo-hoos and blah-blahs and wah-wahs."

"Another good song."

"Play something, anything. Now. Fast."

Daniel started playing an upbeat, funny song that sounded like it could be played at a cattle call.

"You crack me up," she said when he was finished.

As if she needed to validate something he already knew but something very few others knew about him—that he was actually pretty funny when you got to know him.

"We do make a good team, you know," Casey said.

"I know. I think I've always known."

They wrote one more song that day, a funny and quirky song called "The Real Chuck Norris." In the afternoon, as they were getting slap-happy and laughing over everything, Casey said she was tired and wanted to finish up.

"Not with you," she added quickly. "Just here, with these songs. I want to just—I wanna just hang out tonight. Like old times. I want to just be with you. Okay?"

The way she said it made him get nervous and anxious while also making him suddenly want her more than anything. He didn't know what she meant by "just be with you." How did she mean it? Was she referring to more than just sitting next to each other chatting and laughing?

Casey smiled, probably knowing exactly what he was thinking. "I don't want to think about anything tonight— the past or the present or the future. Okay? All I want is to have some fun. To feel light again. And Daniel—I think there's some unfinished business between us. That's overdue. That's long overdue."

* * *

IN HIS MIND, Daniel pictured Casey stepping out of the elevator like a teenager about ready to go to prom. There would be a lightness in her walk, a soft glow on her face. She might be wearing a blush-colored sleeveless top with a matching pleated skirt that looked like a picture of springtime. Daniel would watch her from the chair in the lobby. They would go out to dinner and talk and laugh and enjoy themselves. Then they would lose themselves in the night and the moments and finally be able to lose themselves in each other and finally make up for lost time.

He ordered another beer and sighed as he checked his cell phone again.

Yeah, that would be a nice picture, but of course that couldn't happen.

He looked at the text he'd received an hour after he was supposed to meet Casey for dinner.

> Daniel—I needed to leave. I'm sorry. If I stay around here I don't know what might happen. As much as I've been hurt, I can't do that. To Burke or you. I'm sorry.

He'd double-checked to see if she was still around, but she had already checked out. Just like that.

So much potential and all they managed to come up with was some sad love song and some silly little piece about Chuck Norris.

Such is our story. Such is my life.

He never even got to ask her the question that had been on his mind, the one that he couldn't wait to ask later on that night.

I guess she wasn't gonna kiss me after all.

Just another sad, sappy country song.

I can feel the wind
Before it starts to blow
See the sunrise
Before it starts to glow
I can hear you call
Before you start to dial
I can hear you sentenced
Before you go to trial.
—Sparkland & Winter, "The Real Chuck Norris"

PRESENT DAY

Casey Takes a Chance

I SPENT LAST NIGHT writing and then writing a little more. Now I've spent half a day on Hilton Head trying to do something with that writing.

I've got a plan. I guess, in a lot of ways, I've always had a plan. Sometimes, those plans have backfired. The whole plan to go to Duke and find a career and a man and a future . . . well, I did end up achieving my goals. It's just the final results weren't exactly what I thought they'd be. But are they ever? Does life ever give you exactly what you want or need?

I find a church and ask if I can borrow their piano for just a short while. I explain why, and the receptionist understands. She's a nice elderly woman who takes me to the sanctuary, a small one with just two rows of wooden pews, and tells me to play as long as I'd like.

One of the things I've done since high school is take piano lessons. I still have yet to take guitar lessons, but I keep thinking that one day somebody I used to know might be able to teach me.

It takes me half a day to get my song finished. The final product is rough. Really rough. But the heart and soul of the song are there. Nowadays they can do anything and everything to any song or voice or instrument. What they can't do is use that technology to create something soulful and powerful. You need more than machines to do that. You need people like Daniel. And yeah, you need people like me.

It's amazing to be able to record something on a digital device the size of a pack of chewing gum, then insert it into your computer a little while later and save it. Then that same recording, whatever it might be, can then be sent away to anybody who has an e-mail address. So that's exactly what I end up doing this afternoon. It's that easy and simple.

I don't know what he'll say, but I just hope it means something. I hope it matters.

Daniel Does Something Good

S O WHEN WAS the last time you heard from her?"

I'm sitting with my brother at a table outside the Chicago restaurant we'll be having dinner at. Phil left the office early to meet me for some drinks before his wife and their three kids arrive for a meal and chaos. I'll only be staying for one night with them before heading down south to find out what will happen with my future.

"Remember the country music fest I went to a couple of years ago? Tried to get Heidi and you to come down to?"

"She hates crowds."

"But she loves Lady Antebellum."

"Yeah, well, there was no way we were bringing the kids."

I agree with him on that point. "Doesn't stop some parents. Anyway, that was the last official communication between Casey and me."

"So what—did they not sing her favorite song? Or did you two get into a fight about a song lyric?"

Obviously Phil doesn't know the impact Casey has had on my life. She's that girl who's come up time and time again, but to them she's an afterthought. She's just a good friend. They don't know half the truth, which is fine by me. It's not like me and my brothers have spent a lot of time talking about our girlfriends and our feelings. The only thing that has really brought us together as a unified front has been our collective feelings for our father, the tough drunk who is finally losing his battle with life as his health is starting to decline and the dementia is beginning to set in.

I don't respond to Phil's joke about Casey. I sip a beer and watch a girl in her twenties jog by without an ounce of fat on her lean and mean body. Suddenly I feel the thick and dark IPA I'm drinking, especially around the hula-hoop spare tire of mine that's starting to inflate as time sets in. Maybe I should be jogging instead of drinking.

"So let me get this straight," Phil says in his left-brained, oldest-brother manner. "You just got fired by a company that makes doughnut programs for children. A company you hated working for."

"Plus-one for me," I quickly add.

"Yeah, fine. Now you're going to see a manager who never returns calls to give him a song you still haven't written—"

"I've partially written it."

"*Even* though he already has a whole CD of songs of yours."

"Demos."

"Yeah," Phil says, shaking his head, loving every minute of making my life miserable. "Then you're going to Savannah, right? To find Casey, who you haven't spoken to in two years and who is now making sweet music with her ex-husband?"

"You're really funny."

"That's your plan?"

My brother looks all smug and smirky in the seat across from me, but that's okay, because I'm still better-looking than him and have lots more hair.

"You left out the part about heading back home to go take care of a father who might not remember which son I am. *I* am gonna take care of him."

"Hey—plus-one for you there. He might think you're Jeff."

We've always joked that Jeff, the middle brother, was the one our parents liked the best. They really did smother attention on him. They weren't sure what to do with me, especially my father, who didn't have a single artistic bone or gene in his body.

"So my life plan doesn't quite sound ideal."

Phil laughs. "What are you going to do when you see this girl?"

"Casey."

"Yeah, Casey. What, serenade her on her porch? Or stand outside her ex's house with a boom box in hand playing a Peter Gabriel song?"

"If I have to."

"Please, Daniel. If there's one bit of advice I can give you, *don't* sing."

This is what I've had to put up with ever since starting a band. I know now that I'm not the best singer in the world, but it did take me a while to admit that to myself. I'm not awful, but all those who love me sure like reminding me that I'm really not great.

"So what would you do?"

Phil finishes his beer and looks for the server to come around again. "You don't want to ask me."

"Why?"

"'Cause I envy you. Mr. Single Man. I mean, I love Heidi and I can't imagine being without the kids. But sometimes—you know. I'd love to just take off and drive cross-country."

"You never even used to go on spring-break trips anywhere. You were always working."

Phil thinks about that and nods. "Yeah, you're right. Maybe I'm more like Dad than I'd like to admit."

I see a pretty, dark-haired woman pushing a modern-looking baby stroller down the sidewalk flanked by a boy and a girl. She smiles and waves as Phil stands up and goes to greet them.

"I envy you," I admit to my brother, a bit of truth I normally would have saved for myself.

"I don't know how I'd do it without her," Phil says, loud enough for Heidi to hear.

He hugs her and then embraces his kids. This is obviously a treat for them, seeing their father so early in the day.

As I greet Heidi and the kids, I find myself even more anxious and eager to find Casey. Once and for all. To finally see if there's any remote chance left for us. To finally see if we really do belong with each other or if it's just another fantasy, like this whole song-writing gig I've been trying to tell myself would happen.

I just need to know the truth. That's all. Then I can go my merry little way.

We run toward this cliff called love
But stop just short of being enough
We stare out and see the heights
Then hide away until the rising daylight.
—Sparkland & Winter, "Fall Over" (unpublished)

FED UP AND BROKEN

(2008)

It Comes and It Goes

*T*HE COLD CREPT up and somehow snuck inside this city, releasing a snowstorm and making her isolation all the worse. It didn't help that Daniel kept calling and texting. Nothing about what he did was helping her one bit. Especially since she had not changed a thing in her life since saying she would three years earlier when she saw him in Nashville.

It was a day before December 31 and two before the start of a new year. Casey and Burke were visiting her family in Asheville and would be leaving to go back home on New Year's Day to Savannah. Casey didn't want to think about 2009 because she didn't really want to think much about 2008. Her biggest New Year's resolution the last few years had been ignored and overlooked. It didn't really help when that resolution was out of your hands.

Change your life and your habits.

This had been the goal and the resolution, except it was meant for her husband and not her. Yet Burke was still the same. He went through periods where he tried, in his own way, to change, but then a switch would flip and he'd be that guy again. The distant one who seemed gone a lot, who drank for no reason other than he could, who felt like a stranger both in the kitchen and in bed. This man living with her who made a great income but wasn't particularly great at anything else.

Meanwhile, Casey kept trying to get her life under control. For a while this year, she had started going to church again and reconnecting with some of her friends back there. It wasn't long, however, before the sadness and shame that followed her into the pew made going too much. She didn't feel worthy to be there. Everybody looked at her like she had this perfect and happy life, but inside she felt miserable. Deep down, if Casey were to admit it, she blamed God.

It was easier blaming someone if you didn't have to sit and feign singing songs to Him, or act like you were thanking and worshipping Him.

Another New Year approached, but all the signs pointed to the idea that it was going to be the same year as always. The bleak white snow resembled how she felt in her heart.

And always, in the background, remained Daniel, this constant buzz, this irritating noise her soul couldn't turn off.

He had moved to Denver for some kind of job, and he had told her that before leaving. She wished him luck but that was it. Now he was back in Asheville as well for a week to be with his family for the Christmas holidays. He had been trying for a while to get together with her again. Their last songwriting partnership had produced two hit singles, including the wonderfully throwaway pop song called "The Real Chuck Norris," recorded by Trace Adkins in 2006, and then the sweet love song called "More" perfected by a brand-new group called Lady Antebellum on their debut album. Daniel had wanted to continue the good vibes and success but Casey had been ignoring him.

It was nine at night, and her mom's house that she walked around in felt massive and empty. Burke was at some fund-raiser or charity event—something he hadn't really explained and something she hadn't wanted to go to. She didn't know if he was lying or when he would be getting home. Casey just felt tired and lonely, especially considering her mother was gone and her sisters all had plans.

She finally gave in and called Daniel. Maybe just to say hi or maybe to see how he was doing or maybe to try to ask for help.

"Yeah?" the voice shouted as if in a loud bar.

For a moment, she thought of hanging up, but he would know she was calling. "Hey, Dan, it's me."

"Case?" He was definitely somewhere he could barely hear her. "I've been trying to get hold of you."

"I know. I'm sorry."

"I'm downtown at the Bayou."

A little more noise in that echoing tomb of a house would have been nice, but Casey wasn't quite in the mood for the jazz and blues bar.

"Are you okay?" he asked.

"I'm fine."

"Can I see you before I leave?" he asked.

"When are you leaving?"

"Tomorrow."

"Are you planning on flying?"

"That was the goal. Hopefully it won't snow anymore so I can get out. I have some New Year's Eve plans."

Casey could tell Daniel had been out for a while because his voice sounded a bit different. A bit lighter, a bit more far away. She wasn't sure seeing him would be such a good idea.

"I can meet you anywhere."

"How about Shannon's Pub?"

She had picked a place not far away from the Bayou. A small dive of a pub where she probably wouldn't see anybody she knew. Not that she was hiding anything by going to see Daniel. Just . . .

"That's fine. I'll head over there now."

For a moment she thought about this and then decided seeing him in her current mood wouldn't be the best after all. She had managed to break down last time she saw him.

"Look, Daniel, maybe tonight isn't the best time to get together. We could see each other in the morning if you have time."

But he was already gone, already heading over to Shannon's to meet her there.

She sighed, not sure of what she was going to say when she saw him, not sure of how she could answer some of the questions he surely had for her.

Before leaving, Casey checked her phone to see if Burke had left any messages. Like always, there were none to be found.

Run to You

DANIEL DOWNED ANOTHER beer and knew he needed to slow down even as he hoped Casey would speed up and finally arrive. He had found a booth near the back where they could have some privacy and talk but all he was doing was getting pestered by the server, who wondered when his guest would arrive. Eventually he broke down and texted Casey, only to finally get a response that said she was almost there.

There were so many things he wanted to tell her and he wasn't even sure where to begin. But more than that, he wanted to know how she was doing and what in fact she was still doing with that husband of hers. Daniel knew in his heart that things were still the same. He'd heard some stories from some of his friends who saw Burke out and about, but never with Casey. If things had been going so well for Casey, she would have answered one of his e-mails or phone calls. There had been no responses. Nothing.

Part of him was angry at this silence. Another part, a larger part, was worried, and had been ever since they left each other after meeting in Nashville. He had spent another three years waiting to hear from her, waiting to hear the news that her marriage was over, waiting. But the wait had never ended and the news had never arrived.

Now, he waited again, wondering what he was going to say and how exactly he would say it.

The woman who walked into the pub and found his head sticking out of it wasn't the same one he left in Nashville several years earlier. He hadn't seen her since, not one picture and not one glance. Casey wore a long black overcoat and had dark hair that matched. The sunny springtime Casey seemed permanently gone.

"Changed your hair color again," Daniel said as he greeted her with a hug, noticing she felt more slight than he could remember.

"One day it's probably going to fall out from all the colors it's gone through."

When she took off her coat, he could see just how skinny Casey had become. Probably nothing to be worried about, but certainly not healthy in any way. Her tight jeans didn't seem to have much to work with, and the slender sweater still had room left to be loose. Casey slid into the booth across from where he'd been sitting.

"I haven't been here for a while," she said, glancing around at the subdued crowd.

"Everybody's saving their energy for tomorrow."

"You're headed back to Denver, huh?"

"You remember I live there?"

Casey gave him a knowing look. She looked pale too. Far too pale for his liking. Normally he might have made a vampire joke, but he needed to ease in with the jokes. And the conversation. And basically everything.

"How is your job out there?"

"It's okay," he said.

"What exactly are you doing again?"

"I work for a production studio, where I work on videos."

"Do you write music for them?"

"Sometimes. Not all the time." He paused, smiling. "Not enough."

A look of concern fell over her face.

"I still play. I've got a buddy who I'm playing with. I wouldn't call us a band, but it's something."

"Good."

A server came and took their order. When she left, Daniel couldn't help getting to the point.

"What's been going on with you?"

"School keeps me busy." She looked away as she said that.

"Casey—what's going on? Like really? Why haven't you bothered to respond to one phone call or text?"

"I just couldn't."

"But why? What did I do?"

"You didn't do anything. I just didn't want a series of endless questions like you're doing now."

"My manager has been on me to write more songs. I've tried. I mean, yeah, I've tried, but it's not the same."

"I'm sorry."

Her glass of wine came but she didn't look interested in it. She had probably ordered it just to be polite so Daniel didn't have to drink alone.

"What's going on with you?" he asked again.

"Things are fine."

He waited for more but more didn't come.

Daniel was afraid of this, afraid the same icy chill that hovered outside would arrive with her.

"What happened to all the stuff you said when I last saw you? It's like—it's like that never happened."

"I'm sorry I burdened you with all of that."

He took her cold hand and held it for a moment. "Are you kidding—Casey, it's me. You didn't *burden* me with anything."

She gently slipped her hand away from his. "It wasn't my place—I apologize for that."

"So are things any different? You two are one happy couple or something?"

"Please."

For a moment, Casey seemed to be able to hold back her emotions, but then they leaked out of her. Tears fell and she held a hand in front of her face to stop from showing emotion.

"I'm sorry—this was a bad idea to come—I shouldn't . . ."

"Casey, look at me. Nobody can see you. I'm here. Case?"

She opened her eyes and they were the same. They hadn't aged any and they were still bold and bright and utterly beautiful.

"What can I do?"

"Nothing," she told him.

"I'll do anything."

"You need to leave me alone."

"Are you happy? Are you?"

"It's not your place to ask me that."

"Are you?"

He knew the beer he'd been drinking all afternoon and evening was helping him talk. Good thing too. He didn't want to leave anything unspoken.

"Are you happy?" he asked again.

"Do I look happy?"

"No."

"Well, then, there you go."

For a while there was just silence. He finished his beer and eyed the server to get another.

There were so many things he wanted to say and yet this iceberg of uncertainty weighed down all his thoughts and choices. He couldn't see past it.

"I shouldn't have come." Casey couldn't look him straight in the eyes. Every time they exchanged glances, she would look away.

"I should be more angry, you know."

"Why's that?"

"We have two more hit singles and then—boom. Nothing. I call and I write and nothing. So my career—my job and my dreams—they're all sorta contingent on you. The important piece of the puzzle is you."

"I'm sorry," Casey said.

"Yeah, well, I am too. I'm really sorry. Sorry we ever tried writing songs in the first place. Sorry for getting spoiled by being able to see them amount to something. Sorry for thinking there could be a lot more songs between us."

"That's unfair."

"Is it?"

"Yeah, it is," Casey said, a little more life back in her now as her tone and look changed to anger. "I get enough guilt trips laid on me all the time. Don't you dare lay one on me."

"Oh, okay, sorry. Sorry mine aren't that important."

"I wasn't the one who decided to go pursue your dreams. You remember that? *You* ran away."

"You always remind me, don't you?"

Casey shook her head. "Well, you did. And all these years later, what are you still interested in? The music. The songs. That's all. You just need my help. That's all I am to you."

He cursed. "That's crazy."

"Is it? Is it really?"

He sighed and rubbed his face. He finally got another beer and began working on it.

"I shouldn't have come," Casey said again.

"But you did, so just accept it."

"I didn't come out here to argue. God knows I do that enough back at the house. The times when another human is in the house."

This was insane. This sounded exactly like the Casey Sparkland from several years ago.

"Why don't you leave him?"

"I made a vow."

"To not leave him?"

"Yeah. That's sorta what those wedding vows are. I take them seriously."

"After everything he's done?"

"He's been trying," she said.

Daniel didn't believe her. Casey sounded like she didn't even believe herself.

He couldn't help but let out a loud curse. Casey looked at him, this time with a look of disdain.

"What?" Daniel asked.

"I wonder what it's like to be in love with someone who doesn't have to drink his emotions away. All the important men in my life seem to have that really bad habit."

Daniel felt like he was drowning. Drowning in regret and frustration and confusion. This time he was the one who had the tears falling from his eyes.

"I don't know what else to do with my *emotions* because every single place I go you're there. Do you get that, Casey? You're always there. I wake up and I hear you. I go to work and I think about you. You're the shadow that's always around. I create music to try and figure out a way of expressing those emotions, but I can't articulate them. I need *you* to do that. Which is kinda a catch-22 since your absence is the reason I have those feelings burning a hole through me. So the very least I can do is sit and do what every other male I know does—drink himself silly."

"Daniel—"

She tried to reach out to him, but he pulled his hands away. He could see still the big rock on her finger.

"I'm done," he said, wiping his eyes and trying to be angry enough to stop the pitiful woe-is-me tears.

"Come on—listen, I didn't—"

"It doesn't matter," he interrupted as he cursed and shook his head and gritted his teeth. "It doesn't matter and this doesn't matter and I'm done. You hear that? There are not going to be any more songs and any more e-mails or phone calls or texts, and there's not going to be any more *me* ever again, you got that? Do you?"

"Calm down."

He cursed and looked at her with a gaze that begged for her to look away. "I am tired—*tired*—of chasing you around like some little puppy."

"I never asked you to."

He wanted to say more. Lots more. He wanted to lay into her and rip her apart and make her misery even worse. But he couldn't.

"You're right," he said. "I'm sorry to have asked you to come out here in the first place. Another mistake of mine. But it's the last I make with you. I promise that."

"Daniel . . ."

He stared at the table and couldn't look at her. Not anymore.

The server came and he gave her enough money to cover whatever the bill might be, along with tip and then some. He just wanted to get out of there. He wanted some fresh air and a fresh life.

"I'm not trying to hurt you," Casey said.

"I know. But that doesn't mean you don't. Time and time again."

You want to forgive
But you got a life to live
And you know that life
It's such a beautiful gift.
—Sparkland & Winter, "Settle Yourself"

PRESENT DAY

Daniel Writes a Song

M Y BROTHER'S CONDO is silent as I walk through the large room and look at all the photos on the wall. It reminds me of his old bedroom with all the trophies that used to be on the dresser. It seemed like they kept multiplying as the months went on, and every time I entered his room they'd point at me and start to laugh.

They've left me on my own and I'm procrastinating. I should be trying to work on a song for my manager. You know, the song I'm going to give him when I see him and ask him to help me change my life around. But I'm examining somebody else's life that a voice tells me could've been mine.

Sometimes I wonder what I'm doing here. Wandering around a world I've made for myself with so many songs to sing yet nobody to sing them to.

I wonder what would have happened if I had been a better football player. If I hadn't been drinking and gotten kicked off the team and ended any possible career in the sport. Would I have another life playing a game I love instead of spending my life writing about the games of love? Perhaps I would have been happier or more content.

A profession isn't going to bring peace of mind.

That nagging faith thing echoes like a guitar strumming in the night.

One day.

That's what I've always said.

One day.

But I'm thirty-five years old and one day is today and it's not looking any better. Faith isn't a home-entertainment center you go out and purchase one day. It's not something you suddenly find.

I'm beginning to think it finds you. I've just been locked in this little hole and haven't been found.

Not yet.

This makes me think of Casey. Of course. Everything makes me think of Casey. The glowing moon and the rising sun and all the things in between.

She could help me out.

An excuse, of course.

A crutch, in fact.

One I've used ever since she came into my life. The inability to tell stories or make meaningful music or to even move on in life. Because of Casey.

The girl I turned down not once but twice.

Twice.

Just like your faith.

I go back into the small guest bedroom and pick up my guitar and start strumming. I wander back into the living room to make up some words that say nothing and to hum a song that won't amount to anything. But this is what I do and this is what I need to finally leave behind.

It's time to wise up and move on with life. To settle down.

There are still so many songs I want to sing.

I look at the empty couch across from me. Then I look at the empty notebook pages on the table.

There's still a little more time. Before settling down. My life and my hopes and my dreams can all settle down but my heart will never settle. Never.

The melodies come smoothly and easily. Just like they always have. I pick one and run with it and create another tune. I don't know if it's any good but I don't care. It's another piece of me I've created.

Maybe, if I'm lucky, someone else will one day hear it too.

Casey Makes Her Choice

THE SUN FEELS so good against my forehead. The first touch of every morning gives me a hope that God hasn't forgotten, and neither should I. Those blessings that should be counted. Those promises that should be remembered. Those shadows that should be outrun.

The scent of morning reminds me of joy. The sound of birds reminds me of happiness. The spiraling light coming through the blinds reminds me of better days, of younger days.

I won't see the darkness of night anymore. I won't let it suck me in.

I close my eyes and picture the man I know I love. The way he and I once were, the way it always felt like it could be.

I'm not dreaming or deluding myself. I'm choosing joy. I'm choosing happiness. I'm choosing hope because that's what I have inside of my heart. This dwelling place he once chose to leave behind.

It's a big day for me, and I close my eyes for a moment to pray the prayer I so desperately need.

"Give me the right words to say to Burke and help me know I'm making the right decision."

I know love is patient and kind. But love also acts. Love doesn't always have to wait around.

I'm not settling for second place anymore and I'm not letting love sit in the backseat. I'm going to drive toward my future and finally bury the past and be okay with that choice since today is all I know I have.

Daniel's Demise

I'M DRIVING TOWARD my destiny in Nashville when the guy holding it in his hands sends me an e-mail. I'm driving on the freeway and know better but I open up the message on my iPhone. I can't help it. Every part of me is anxious because I know I don't have some magnificent song written. I have a decent demo and that's it. A decent demo with a lot of willpower and heart. I just want to sit across from Gary Mains and force him to be a little uncomfortable. I want him to have to look and listen to me as I talk about dreams and about desires and about having to wait.

The message is short and sweet:

Hey D!

Something came up and I'm out of the office this week. So sorry. Would've loved to have seen you. Let's try to set up another time when I'm back.

Gary

I want to pull off the side of the interstate and quietly throw up my morning's breakfast.

I guess the good news is he told me he wasn't going to be at his office instead of having me show up and wait.

Call him. Call him and demand a meeting.

Yeah, that'll work. That'll work because I'm certainly the one calling the shots here, right? I'm certainly the one the world is waiting for.

I let out a curse.

I think of something a youth pastor once told me when I questioned his idea of faith.

God has plans for you, Daniel.

I didn't know that *Dandee Donuts* fit into God's plan. Nor did my songwriting demise.

In a way, I shouldn't have to worry anymore. Gary might as well be saying he's through with me. He doesn't have the guts to actually come right out and end things, because who knows when and if I might write some beautiful song the world will embrace. He wants to hedge his bets, like they all do. Like every single-selling soul does.

Again, that awful urge comes. To call a number I don't know. To talk to a soul I've lost touch with. It's the Casey from high school and college who I want, not the current Casey.

I think of other scenarios, but none seem to make any sense. The only thing that makes sense now is to return home to a father who won't recognize me and then help him slowly die. Perhaps I'll write songs of misery and torture that amount to something. Maybe I'll just get really fat and lazy and end up working at a cheese factory.

The bigger the dreams, the harder you might fall when you don't achieve them. Right? So don't have them. Is that what I should tell someone? Because I can't. I don't believe that.

The dreams count. They mean something. This road and journey has all meant—something. I'm simply waiting for an explanation and an outcome.

Do you hear me, God? I'm not demanding. I'm just asking. Pleading. Begging for a little break.

The world twists and turns and sometimes I wonder how few ever stop to see this treadmill.

People applaud the arrival but don't bother noticing the journey.

People cheer the coronation but don't wonder who put together the ceremony.

These dreams are like train tracks that can take you far away from this place. One by one by one by one. Nobody but you can count them all. Nobody knows how far you've come when you arrive. If you arrive.

The where is what I want to know. The when is what I want to touch. But the why is the one thing I've known all my life. The why is the reason I struggle so much.

A song is just another way to speak the truth. Lyrics are just another form of therapy. I narrate this life and this story and yet I fear never seeing or hearing the outcome. Sometimes I wonder if this is the outcome and if life is always going to look a little like this.

Casey and Burke

I PULL UP TO the driveway that could've been mine and face
the house that I just signed away a couple of days ago. But I
know that these can still be mine if I want them. This drive and this
home and this life can still be mine if I choose for them to be.

If I choose the safe and easy way.

I didn't fall in love with the monster who came in the middle
of the night. I fell in love with a handsome football player named
Burke who carried his sweet Southern charm as effortlessly as he
threw the ball. He held dreams and allowed me to dream some
too: for children, for a happy life, for security, for fulfilling days.

The inability to have children was a blow, something that took us both by surprise and something we didn't talk about too much. In between his drinking and cheating, I doubted I even wanted to have this man's child. But when we specifically tried, we had nothing to show for it.

Those dreams aren't entirely gone. I know that as I step out of the car again and walk up to the doors of this stunning home. Maybe the man I married is like this house. His past is like the old mansion that once belonged to his family, the one that got burned down. Maybe this new structure is like the man inside, wanting and hoping and dreaming to start over again.

I take a slow breath and steady my nerves.

Burke.

He opens the door and then embraces me, thanking me for coming. He called earlier to ask if we could see each other. I told him I'd be here soon enough.

"I didn't think you were going to come," he tells me.

He doesn't look as pale as he did the first time I saw him. The glow is back on his face, just like it had been on the beach.

Maybe we can just fall into each other's arms and make love and end the story like some passionate over-the-top romance novel.

I am a true Southern girl, a romantic, but I never have lived in that story. My story hasn't always been linear, or easy to explain, or simple to understand.

"I've been thinking a lot about everything you've said. About everything, to be honest."

Burke puts his hands together, his bright-blue polo shirt contrasting with his white pants. "Me too."

"Let's go inside."

"Do you have good news or bad news?" he asks with a smile.

"I have great news. I no longer want to remember the things we can't undo and can't go back and change. I don't want to be stuck the rest of my life, Burke."

"I don't either."

He looks surprised and unsure and slightly taken aback.

"Come on, let's go inside and chat," I tell him, taking his hand.

When you strip away the brokenness inside this man, there's so much to love about him. I guess the same thing can be said about anyone, including me.

Especially me.

We walk inside the hallway to go talk. I know the things I want to say. I just am not sure exactly how I'll say them all.

It's always—always—easier writing things down. Or, at least it is for me.

Daniel Back Home

I'VE BEEN DRIVING all day and the summer sun is slowly starting to nod off as I drive down a dusty road to the house I grew up in. I'm listening to the radio belt out some Jimmy Buffett and I think about all the songs I heard driving over these rocks and ruts. How many times did I have my hand outside a window and wonder where I was going to be in ten or twenty years?

That's the beauty of music.

The stories of every pop or country song ever sung are potential and promise. The potential of finding that special someone. The promise that tomorrow will no longer be as lonely as today. The songs lift you up and make you brave as you go out into the dark night in search of love and belonging. Then the songs comfort you as you come back home alone and tired.

The songs I used to sing as a twentysomething seem to mock me now. I want to go back in time and rewind the tape, yet there are no tapes to be found. Only digital recordings, things that exist but can't be seen or touched. Like this unseen promise of love, like all that wasted potential I used to have.

Is thirty-five really that old? Because I still feel young.

Can I still find the love promised so long ago? Can I still live up to the potential I once believed I could fill?

I want to believe in a simple melody complex enough to move the masses. I want to strive for a simple chorus memorable enough to be sung in the stadiums. A love song that makes up for those long nights and those lost days. A lovely song filling in the grays with blues and making the melancholy go away.

I slow down as I get to the dirt driveway. It winds around the trees and back toward the sloping hill. I've been gone too long. So long, yet I haven't really managed to get very far.

I can see the sun glowing on the edge of my old house. It's small and quaint but it is like one of the longed-for songs. This little cabin has got some soul. The memories are too many to be fully told. Sad to say, inside sits a man with very few memories to conjure up. The tales and the songs are beginning to be erased by time itself.

I sigh and then grab my phone, thinking maybe Gary changed his mind or maybe Casey miraculously called. But no, my phone doesn't show that I've won the lottery yet.

I get ready to see my father. He's surely not ready in any way to see me.

I'm not the same one you ran from
I'm not the same soul you tried to make whole
Courage isn't commitment but cutting the cord
Being the brave one has never been my goal.
—Sparkland & Winter, "Settle Yourself"

CRISSCROSSING

(2009–2011)

Little Unlucky at Love

*I*T WAS A little after midnight and Casey wished she could open a window and slide out of it to go sit on the rooftop. But this roof was so steep that she would probably fall and break her neck. She missed her old house in Biltmore Forest. She missed the house she and Burke moved into in Savannah when they first married. She missed—she missed a lot of things.

The suitcase was packed, yet she couldn't zip it up. That felt too final. She still hoped Burke would come home. She had no idea where he was. There had been a business dinner. Business dinners didn't last till midnight, but the ones Burke went to surely did. She'd had enough.

A part of her felt like it couldn't breathe. She had gone over this time and time again. There were the exterior things, like what others would think and what their friends would say and what her life would suddenly begin to look like. Those things didn't matter as much as the interior things, like how her heart felt dried up like a prune and impossible to soften, like how her soul felt stuck in the shadows. She knew God didn't want her leaving, but she had tried everything. She had a right to, right? But something in her told her to stick it out. Another part of her told her that if she left she would be alone the rest of her life.

I'm alone now. What's the difference?

She could hear the cool April breeze coming through a window. She should at least get a puppy. Some kind of companion, even if it was small and furry. She needed it for that shriveled-up heart and soul. She needed it for her sanity.

I'm so angry and I'm so tired of being so angry.

She zipped up her suitcase. A box of miscellaneous things she had collected from drawers and her closet sat next to the suitcase on the bed. It included pictures and song lyrics and the CD Daniel had given her.

She didn't want to think of Daniel now. He had no part of this. He was not part of *this* story. Yes, he had called her earlier and yes maybe he had suddenly gotten her attention.

But maybe he's the reason this story is happening.

She shoved the thought away. Daniel was not the reason Burke was a drunk and a cheater. Daniel had nothing to do with Burke's character and his behavior.

But maybe you didn't give enough of yourself to Burke the way you once did with Daniel?

Again, the voice was ridiculous and out of line. There was a difference between a high school sweetheart and a husband of several years. People changed. The honeymoon eventually ended. Making love eventually turned into something that felt like it had to be remade over and over again. Or it eventually turned into memories of making it.

She wanted to leave this life behind. Casey had endured enough.

It's not going to be easy.

She knew that. She didn't know how hard it might be, but it was time to leave. It was time to figure out a new dream. It was time to stop needing some kind of worn-out blanket covering her. She could take the cold, because God knew she had taken everything else.

My Lucky Day

*T*HE TEXT CAME on his first date with Sheryl Miller. They had just been getting together for coffee, so maybe it wasn't an official date. Daniel hadn't really dated that much over the years, so he still wasn't sure what a real date looked like. But Sheryl was interested in him and had said so and had simply wanted to get together for coffee and chatting. He had read the text when she had excused herself to use the ladies' room.

It had come from one of the guys in his band who still lived around Asheville, a guy named Hicks who sent him a dirty joke every so often via text.

Casey and Burke getting a divorce. Did u know?

They had been married since 2002. Seven years. Seven very long years.

Maybe Daniel shouldn't have known this, but he knew it too well.

The news came as a surprise. Not a shock. No, nothing with Casey could ever shock him unless she got hurt or killed. No, this wasn't a shock. But he was still surprised to hear about it.

The tall figure of Sheryl whisked by and sat in the comfortable seat next to him.

"Have you ever jumped out of a plane?"

For a moment, Daniel wondered if she was talking to him. "What?"

"Skydiving. Ever done it?"

"No. The thought of plunging to the ground from an airplane with a backpack full of strings and cords and a chute—yeah, that's never really tempted me."

"Wouldn't it be fun to learn together?"

Daniel laughed. "No. Going to a concert is fun. Drinking coffee is fun. Skydiving seems insane."

"What if I told you I had two gift certificates to go?"

"I'd say tell me when you go and I'll bring some binoculars to watch."

Sheryl grinned. "You're funny, you know that?"

"I've been told."

"Well, I just thought it would be something unique to do. To tell the kids one day."

"The kids. Wow. You leave to go to the bathroom and suddenly I'm skydiving and having children."

"They both seem to be in the same category," she said, then quickly added "and who said I was talking about *you* with the kids?"

"You're pretty blunt," he said.

"I've been told."

It was easy to forget the news while at this coffee shop in Denver miles away from Casey and Burke and Asheville and those stories.

Easy for the moment.

THAT NIGHT, HE sent Casey a simple text.

I heard. I'm sorry.

He waited for a response, but a response didn't come.

Jesus, Take the Wheel

GOD BLESS HER family. Her sisters and her mother and, yes, even her father, who still failed but tried so hard with her. They were all there the days and weeks and months after she left Burke. Nobody judged her. They comforted her and made her laugh. Yet still, a chunk of her was missing. She couldn't buy back those years and the wasted time and the huge empty hole inside of her.

A year after leaving Burke, after she moved back to be near her family in Asheville, Casey got a new job at a high school teaching English. She began to go to church with her mother. She reconnected with friends. Things felt like they should have been fine.

She was moving and staying busy, but a part of her remained unglued and undone. A part of her remained stuck somewhere. She just didn't want to look behind her to try to figure out where that somewhere might be.

There were weeks of battling it out with God. Not saying *Your will be done* but wondering where He might be in the midst of all this. Things felt very silent when it came to God. Very silent.

Throughout, there would be a nagging little itch somewhere inside, reminding her about the potential and possibility. This guy named Daniel. This guy who had remained single and had remained quite interested in her. This guy who today, on this first day of October, had texted her again:

You doing okay?

She either needed to answer him or change her phone number. Enough standing in the middle of the field. Enough refusing to be on either side and either team. Either she was going to try to be on Team Daniel or she needed to get back on Team Denial and start racing hard.

You're not a teenager and this isn't a vampire novel and too bad it isn't.

Burke was the vampire who had sucked her dry. Her heart and soul with a long kiss.

She wondered what happened to the old Casey, the one who refused to mope and sit around and wait. She was hiding. That's what she was doing. Hiding and not doing a thing about her life.

She decided to do something.

She grabbed her phone and answered Daniel's text:

> I feel like writing ten thousand songs.

She knew what she was saying in that simple reply. In just a mere few minutes, Daniel sent her another message:

> All I need is my guitar. You name the date and the time.

Just like that, she wasn't hiding anymore. She was in the middle of the field. She had the ball again and she was starting to move toward the goal line.

But what's a touchdown look like?

Casey didn't want to answer that, not yet. She simply wanted an easy and carefree first down. That would be it.

The men in her life would've been so proud of her for thinking in football-talk.

Don't Come Around Here No More

O F COURSE HE shouldn't have accepted. Of course he should have told her the news before he went back to Asheville. The news about falling for this girl in town named Sheryl and the fact that he had given her a ring. But in his mind, he was working. This was about the possibility of getting his songwriting career back on track. Yes, it involved Casey, and yes, there were still feelings there because there would always be feelings. But this had been about work.

So why didn't you tell Sheryl the truth?

He wasn't hiding anything. He just didn't want her worrying.

You don't want her to know.

Daniel hated these little conversations with himself. No matter how loud the music might be, those voices would always be whispering in his mind and soul.

When he knocked on the same door he knocked on when he was a teenager, Daniel felt young again. Young and silly and stupid. Casey answered, looking older and wiser and somehow more beautiful.

"Oh, I was looking for Casey Sparkland," he told her.

She smiled. "Hi, Daniel."

"How do you know my name? This woman I'm looking for— things have been rough for her. She's fallen on hard times. I've heard her hair has fallen out and she's gained about two hundred pounds."

"That's not nice. What if I had?"

"You would still be unmistakably Casey."

He didn't want to say that meant she would always be beautiful and always be charming and always be loved.

He didn't even want to admit that to himself.

"Thanks for coming," she said.

"Thanks for letting me."

She had a brightness in her eyes that he couldn't remember seeing the last couple of times he had been with her. Maybe getting rid of the dead weight was a good thing for her.

What about your weight, Daniel? Huh? Gonna tell her sometime soon?

"Would you like to come in?"

"Um, yeah, sure."

"Don't worry—my mother isn't around. I told her you were coming over and she decided to have dinner with some friends."

Daniel felt a hundred pounds lighter. "So, I can tell she's still a big fan of mine."

"I don't know if she'll ever be. Come on—my sisters are inside. Prepare to be abused."

"Sparklands are all the same," he said.

"Yes, we are."

"PLAY ME A song," Casey said.

They had gone outside after dinner and were sitting on the back deck of her house. Casey wanted to get started right away, finally seeming ready and able to provide him a hundred lyrics to a hundred songs.

"Ready to make some sweet music?" she asked with a sly grin.

"I'm ready to try."

But Daniel really wasn't ready. Nothing came out, especially nothing new. Casey seemed to notice this so she told him to just play some songs for her.

He started with a Beatles song and just played it, not singing it. He realized it was "Something," so he changed it to something else. Something less lovey-dovey. But the next song that came out was "God Only Knows" by the Beach Boys, which was probably even worse.

"I detect a theme here," Casey said, announcing the obvious.

"I haven't written a song in a while, to be honest," he said to her, putting down his guitar.

"Well, I'll help you out, then. Let's do 'The Pi Song Part 2.' Or another song about Chuck Norris."

He sighed and looked at her backyard.

"What's wrong? Is it because you're here? Something to do with my mom?"

Daniel needed to tell her the truth. Before doing something so real and raw and personal as writing music together.

"I'm engaged."

For a moment, Casey appeared to be trying to understand what it meant.

"You know, like engaged to be married," Daniel continued.

She blinked a few times and nodded, politely smiling. "That's great."

"I just felt like I needed to tell you before—"

"Before I try to seduce you and put a ring on your finger and get us both to the altar, right?"

He shook his head. "No, I didn't mean that, it's just—"

"It's fine. You say it like it's some deep, dark confession. I'm happy for you, Daniel."

He hadn't expected her to be so casual and calm about it.

Maybe I don't want you to be happy for me.

"Then let's write some love songs, okay?" she said. "Perfect time to do it."

Daniel didn't necessarily agree, yet he nodded and picked his guitar back up. It suddenly felt heavier. As he glanced over at

Casey, she wore a perplexed yet amused look on her cute face.

"What?"

"Nothing. You just—you never cease to surprise, Mr. Winter."

"Neither do you."

"Let's at least get warmed up," Casey said. "Something magical might happen."

That was what he was afraid of. And what he so desperately wanted.

THE NEXT DAY, it took Casey to name the elephant in the room.

"So what are we doing here?"

Daniel looked up from where he was sitting. He'd been playing his guitar in a zombielike mode. He wasn't even aware that Casey was waiting on him to try to figure out a chorus.

They were in a small recording studio that was located behind a small cabin not far from the city. Daniel knew the musician/producer who owned it and asked for a favor. Just a little time. It wasn't being used, and they only needed it for the privacy and for the keyboard.

"We're trying to come up with some songs."

"Is that it?" Casey said. "Really? Seriously?"

She looked so young, still after all this time, still filling the space with her words, still relying on Daniel to give her an answer. Like so many times before, he was speechless. Nobody had ever made him more speechless than Casey Sparkland.

"Because I can leave now if that would be easier."

"What are you talking about?"

"Daniel—you can barely look me in the eye. It's like—it's all of a sudden like we're back in high school again."

"I could look you in the eye."

"Okay, fine, then it's worse."

"It's just a bit—I don't know. Things are different."

"I'm not doing anything," Casey said. "I'm just being myself."

Yeah, being yourself talking about broken people and failed love stories. All while I can't help but think only about you.

Daniel knew this was one of those defining moments you had, the kind you take for granted when you're younger, the kind you seek to find when you're older.

We're in the middle point, I think, on the teeter-totter of life, wondering which way it will fall next.

"I don't know what else to say to you," Casey said. "You've sorta shut down."

Daniel nodded and looked at her. He stared at her strawberry spirals and wondered how this would turn out. Casey had made her choice and her decision. He could reach for her hand and she could take his and they could start walking into the sunset, hoping for happiness. Or he could remain distant and watch her eventually walk away and always wonder what could have been. Or maybe Casey could walk away and then turn around to glance at him one last time then step over onto the street and get slammed by an oncoming bus.

He really hoped that last ending wasn't the outcome.

"I never really expected you to say yes when I asked to get together," he told her.

She stood and walked across the room to grab a bottle of water. "This is just like a repeat of every track on every single awful record we've played."

She was still talking, and she'd continue to.

"Just tell me and we can stop," Casey said.

"No. Let's keep going. I'll just—I'll get a little more comfortable as we go on. Okay?"

She looked at him and smiled and already he felt a little better.

I Couldn't Love You More

I'M NOT LETTING *him go, not this time, not today.*

At some point during their sessions Casey told herself this. Perhaps she was being selfish or thoughtless, but it was time to be a little selfish or thoughtless. It was time to be a bit reckless when all she'd ever been was careful. Careful to make sure she didn't end up alone. Careful to make sure she ended up with the right guy.

Maybe it didn't make any sense, the two of them together, after all this time. Maybe he really was engaged and maybe he really did love that girl. But Casey didn't buy it. Not a bit. It was time to finally chase the guy who'd been chasing her so many years.

She made it clear through one of the songs they were creating.

"He sings with his soul but loves with his head. So cautious and careful to be full of regret."

These weren't just any ordinary lyrics. Just any ordinary song.

"She whispers for him to come near. She wonders what's keeping him there."

At that line, Daniel stopped playing music and just looked at her.

"What?"

"Interesting lyrics," he said.

"That's why I'm here, right? To keep them interesting."

"That's an understatement."

DAYLIGHT DISAPPEARED AND the time in the studio felt like it was on permanent pause, yet Casey liked that. They had come up with a few songs, all halfway decent, but nothing that really stood out. Yet Daniel didn't seem to mind. He appeared comfortable taking his time. They laughed a lot. Conversations began and shifted and morphed. Soon she noticed it was evening, and Daniel suggested grabbing some pizza and working a little more.

Work involved eating pizza with the works and drinking red wine and talking about the past decade. Casey graduated college in 2000, the same year Daniel would have if he had stayed in school. This was how the conversation started, with her talking about her ten-year-reunion and Daniel talking about possibly trying to finish up school one day.

This was how Casey knew it was right to be there with Daniel, that it was right to feel what she felt inside. It just felt like they could have talked for the rest of their lives. It was so effortless and so easy and it put her weary soul at ease. Maybe that's what a relationship should do. Maybe it shouldn't be about the heavy passion and the rush of emotion but rather about the weightlessness and silent stillness. Maybe it's just about being and hanging out and being okay with that.

Conversation drifted to her marriage and Burke, but Casey didn't dwell on it. Daniel spoke about his job in Denver and about Sheryl but he spoke about those things in a distant way. Not in the way he might speak about Springsteen's latest album or about, well, anything to do with them.

At one point in the evening-turning-into-night, Casey lounged on the floor facing Daniel, who was spread over a couch laughing hysterically and wiping tears off his face while recounting a story about running into someone from their high school class. For a moment she felt this overwhelming waterfall of emotion. For a moment, she had to stop herself from crying.

Daniel noticed it and gave her a funny look. "What?"

She only shook her head.

"No, what? What's wrong?"

"Nothing."

He sat up, looking confused and surprised. "What? What'd I say?"

"No, it's nothing."

"Case, seriously—what'd I say?"

"You didn't say or do anything. I'm just—I'm just taking this in. All of it."

"All of what?"

"All of you. All of us. All of *this,* sitting here without a care in the world and laughing and eating and talking."

"Should we start working?"

Sometimes Daniel could be so clueless. "No, we shouldn't start working."

"Then what?"

"Let me just enjoy this, okay?" she said to him.

He still didn't quite understand what she was feeling, but neither did she. Yet she didn't want to reason and she didn't want to think about yesterday or tomorrow. She just wanted to be in this warmth and laugh and enjoy Daniel and enjoy herself. That was all. That was everything.

Ring and Lionheart

*I*T WAS LATE and it seemed the glow of dinner had started to fade. Casey seemed tired, but more than that, her mood seemed to start to shift. Daniel thought that whatever she had been feeling earlier had started to slip away, like she was second-guessing herself. Again.

"Okay, I'm going to ask, again," he said to Casey as she sat on the edge of the leather couch holding an empty wineglass. "What's going on?"

"I can't just dive back into these waters."

"Who says you're diving in?"

Her eyes pierced him with a knowing look. "Anything to do

with you involves the deep end. There's nothing shallow going on here."

"I can be shallow."

"I'm not talking about you, Daniel. I'm talking about us. And I just got done with an 'us' that didn't turn out so good."

"That's been a year."

"It still feels like it's been just a few days. I mean—think about it. We've been talking about high school like it just happened."

"There's nothing to worry about."

"I don't want to lose anything else," Casey said. "I've already lost enough."

"The best love songs are about losing it all."

Casey chuckled. "Then we're a whole collection of them."

"I still love you." He said this without thinking or hesitating.

"I know."

"And that doesn't matter?"

"Why should it matter, because it's always been the same. Yesterday and yesteryear and every yesterthing I can think of. There's *you*. Yesteryou."

"That should be a song title."

She sat up and put her glass on the table. "This isn't a pop song and we're not starring in a high school musical. This is my life and I want it back. I want you to stop hijacking it."

Daniel walked over and knelt beside her on the floor. "I'm not doing anything. You agreed to come here."

"You're being. You're here. You're there. Right across from me."

"We're working."

"No, we're not," Casey said. "These sessions—you know exactly what you're doing."

"No, I don't."

"You're engaged, yet you want to see if there's any chance and any hope that there still might be something with us. Right? Tell me if I'm wrong."

"And what—there's not? It sure seems like there's still something."

"There's always been something," Casey said, standing up and walking across the room. "You're getting me to tell you every single thing that's going on in my life."

"I can't help that you write from the heart," Daniel said as he followed her to the keyboard and the chair Casey sat on.

"You don't have to keep asking me to come and help you write songs."

"You don't have to keep saying yes," he said.

She looked at him and shook her head. "I should've never agreed to come."

"Stay."

"And what? What's the endgame here, Daniel?"

"A great song."

"That's all you want? A great song?"

He stood next to her and looked long and hard at her. "When you write one, you know you can do it again."

"I don't know if sparks can happen again."

Daniel smiled. "They're already happening."

"Don't give me that look."

"I'm not giving you any look."

"Don't—stay over there."

He took his hand and stroked her cheek. He just wanted to see if she and this were real and not some dream.

"Why? Why are you so frightened?" he asked.

"I'm not frightened of anything. I think I should go."

Casey stood but Daniel gently held her arm, guiding her toward him. She didn't want to go anywhere and they both knew it.

"You're shaking." He held her in his arms and for a moment, she let him.

Daniel moved his head close to hers, but she tried to move hers away. Yet she remained there, in his arms, below him, safe and secure. Daniel couldn't help smiling, looking down into her eyes and making sure they didn't look away.

"You're okay," he said. "The world's not going to end if you let me hold you."

"You shouldn't even be here. Daniel—you're engaged and I'm just—"

"I've been thinking that was probably a mistake," he said.

"Yeah, men have a habit of making mistakes like that."

"Don't put the mistake of others on my shoulders. I'm not Burke."

"Yeah, but I know who you are, Daniel Winter."

"Casey Sparkland?" he asked her, moving his head closer to hers, the smile still there.

"Don't." She was so unconvincing.

"Are you gonna—" Daniel began.

"Stop it."

"Kiss me—"

"Daniel."

"Or not?"

Daniel kissed her and felt the ground disappear and felt the past decade dissipate. He felt young and hopeless and helpless and loved. He felt like he belonged right there.

They kissed again and it felt like their first kiss and their last kiss and all the ones in between as time stopped but Daniel didn't.

Fragile

A BLINK AND THE next day became a week. Another blink and a week became a month.

Somehow, the memory of those kisses didn't fade, but Casey was still strong enough to push Daniel away. He was in another state. He was in another life. And right after he had left, she had felt guilt at kissing someone who was engaged, and also anger that he had gone there. She was reminded of Burke and of all the hurt he had caused, and she began to feel something similar when Daniel didn't call. Soon she woke up and realized this was not going to be her life. This was not going to be her story.

She didn't tell Daniel this. Not right away.

In the course of a year, Daniel had broken up his engagement and started talking about moving back to Asheville. She reminded him not to give up on his musical dreams, but sometimes it seemed like the only dream he had involved her. It worried her, because Casey didn't know.

She was scared.

No, she was terrified.

What if the dream became reality?

What if their story ended up fading out and becoming like one of those albums you never bothered to listen to ever again?

What if the Casey who Daniel had put on this pedestal was suddenly discovered for who she really was?

A new year came and little by little she tried building a bigger wall between her and Daniel.

She thought she was sending him a message. She assumed he understood she wasn't ready and probably would never be.

Yet in the late spring of 2011, she received two tickets in the mail from Daniel. One was for a plane, and the other was for a concert.

Holding them in her hand, she had wept. Silently and alone. These were symbols of a future. She knew that. But she wasn't ready. She wasn't even close to being ready. All she could think about was her own mother and father. Or herself and Burke. Or all the others out there who had never made it last. Who had married the dream and then realized the reality was much different.

She had prayed for help and wisdom and for something, anything.

She didn't know how to say yes even though everything in her wanted to say no.

Need You Now

H E HAD NOT heard from her since he sent the tickets. It was obvious what she was doing and how she
was feeling, but Daniel refused to give up. At least, right after
he had dropped them in the mail. Yet as summer came and
as the date approached, he tried contacting her. He tried reaching out.

A week before, he sent one final text to her:

I'm still planning on going and planning on being
there in Nashville. And I want you to be there too.
I'll be waiting.

It hadn't been some kind of ultimatum. He was still offering hope and still offering them a chance. In his mind, this would have gone so differently, but that was the way things went with Casey. Everything would have gone differently if it had been up to him.

The unfortunate thing about relationships is there are two people involved, and each one has a choice to do whatever they want.

The day of the show came, and Daniel only found continued silence from Casey. He had arrived in Nashville early that Friday morning. He arrived at the CMA Music Festival on his own.

It was ironic he was somewhere hosted by the Country Music Association and Casey wasn't anywhere around.

He waited and wondered if Casey might surprise him.

He still hoped. Even by midday, after not hearing a single thing, he held out hope.

After all this time, he still held it.

CASEY WOULD HAVE liked this. Not the massive crowd of people, Daniel knew, but the band playing. All the groups playing at the fan fair on LP Field during the lead-up to the Country Music Awards. All the big names would be playing there that weekend—Dierks Bentley, Reba, Sugarland, Trace Adkins, The Band Perry, Keith Urban, Taylor Swift. The list was endless. Anybody who had ever sung Sparkland & Winter songs was there that weekend.

That was why he had done it. Why he'd wanted to surprise Casey.

They were a tiny part of this event. This music was a tiny part of the reason they were together.

A tiny and a huge part.

Yet as Daniel sat watching Lady Antebellum performing at night, something happened. It was during their song "More" when a switch got turned. Like the brilliant lighting that was used during the show, and the massive screens behind the band, something bright and brilliant went off in his heart.

Daniel finally realized that he'd had enough.

Daniel finally knew it was okay to let her go.

He had tried. That night was supposed to be some kind of grand statement about their tomorrows. The songs were going to speak to *them*. Yet instead they spoke to him. One lone, solitary figure in a sea of strangers.

Lady Antebellum sang the lyrics *"We dance to feel whole knowing there's gotta be more."* The lyrics Casey had written so many years ago.

Lyrics that suddenly spoke to Daniel more than they ever had before.

There's gotta be more, but I'm not gonna find it here.

As Lady Antebellum changed songs and began to sing their biggest hit, Daniel made his decision. He grabbed his phone and sent Casey one more text. One last text.

Lady Antebellum is singing "Need You Now"
but you wanna know something?

For the first time in my life, I don't need you now.

Now or ever again.

With the music still playing, Daniel walked off into the night, no longer wondering and waiting for something special to come his way.

If you won't settle for more
Then I won't settle for less
I'm not some revolving door
In a pretty little dress.
—Sparkland & Winter, "Settle Yourself"

PRESENT DAY

Daniel Dreams of Four Minutes

MY FATHER IS sleeping in the big hospital bed in his bedroom and the nurse has left for her lunch break. I sit in Dad's old armchair and swear I can still smell the meat loaf I used to make drifting around, even though it's been years since I made it. Maybe just being here reminds me of those smells and those times. Just Dad and me and meat loaf pie.

I've been here for a day and I know I need to try to ease my restless mind. I can't help but think about leaving Seattle, about the news that Casey has gone back to Burke, the reality that I no longer have a manager (or any semblance of a career, either). I think about the letter I sent and feel like an idiot.

I stare at the old record player in the corner of the room. I wonder if it still works. The records are all below, lined up one after another, with all their songs and all their hits just waiting to be listened to. I kneel down and start taking out all these records. For the first time, I realize that this love of music is something I inherited from my father.

Yet he gave it up like some youthful bad habit.

I notice the albums. So many classic ones. Bob Dylan and Elvis and Sinatra. I realize he's got a wide variety of tastes—or at least he used to when he still listened to music.

For a moment I think of my father, zonked out in his bed. He was once young, and the world surely felt big and bright for him. But then . . . well, life happened. Maybe the music reminded him too much of that big and bright world out there. Maybe it was better to keep the records down below and keep the music off.

I pick up the Beatles' *Revolver* album and study it. I think of all the hits they made—hundreds, right? So many beautiful and mesmerizing songs.

Just one. That's all I've ever asked for. All I've ever really wanted. Four minutes of perfection. Four minutes of beauty. Something to share with the rest of the world.

I remember something my manager Gary once said to me. It only takes four minutes to change your life. That's all it takes. Yet I've lived almost four decades trying to go for four minutes. Sure, I've managed to have a few hit songs, but that's always been with my sunshine of a partner, my little soul sister who's no longer there.

Four minutes. I want to laugh. Sometimes I wonder if I only have a minute inside of me. Or maybe two? You know?

I know magic isn't something you can create, but I believe you do what you can to try to make it. The same way you put one and one together to make two. It's not always that simple and easy, but sometimes it's just that.

The album in my hand is a piece of history and a snapshot of yesterday, but it reminds me of something.

Sometimes the magic works.

Sometimes it's that simple and easy.

You put one and one together to make two. To make something beautiful. To make something perfect.

I think what I want, what I *really* want, is four minutes more with Casey. Just four more minutes to make a little more.

There are chords we haven't created yet. There are songs we haven't begun to sing.

There are clichés I haven't even tried to cash in on yet.

There are moments we can make.

So go on and get those four minutes. Or at least see if you have any time to spare.

I sigh and glance out the window. Then I'm up and I'm heading out the door.

An angry text sent from an outdoor concert is no way to tell the love of your life good-bye. I don't know a lot of things in this world, but I know I need to end things in a more proper way.

I need to go find Casey once again. Even if she's already decided her future, for the second time.

Casey Believes in the Dream

IT'S BEEN A long time."

I sit on the stone wall and look out toward the valley below. I'm reminded how often I used to have conversations like this when I was a teen. When the world didn't make me so weary. When life didn't always feel so long.

"I'm sorry I've tried doing it on my own."

The wind blows around me. The clouds look like balled-up swans in the sky, sleeping on the clear blue water. I know my voice is heard loud and clear though I'm the only one sitting here on the lookout point on the Blue Ridge Parkway.

"Please let me know I've made the right decision. Please help

him—and help me—understand You more. I just can't—I can't do this on my own, God. But I can't rely on some other broken soul to lift me up either."

The gust of wind seems to answer my requests. But maybe that's just the wind, nothing more.

I think back to the choice I've made, to the things I've done, to the door I've opened to my past and to my future. Yes, he's a messed-up man, and yes, it won't be perfect. But I believe we can make it work. With God's help we can make us work.

The past only seems to be a stone's throw away. If thrown right, I could skip it off the smooth surface of the sky. If tossed perfectly, perhaps I could find myself seventeen again with the world at my feet. Would I make the choices I made then? Would I do the things I did? Would I try to make a different life from the one I already have?

I would believe in those childhood dreams, as outlandish as they might be.

Nobody ever showed me they could amount to anything. Nobody ever proved that they could still keep dreaming once they've become a full-time adult with full-time responsibilities. Nobody except Daniel.

I wonder where he is. I wonder if he's looking up at those same clouds.

I hope he's still dreaming.

I hope the dreams haven't died inside of him.

At least, not all of them.

Daniel Looks for an Answer

WHAT ARE YOU doing here?

A chorus of voices might ask this.

Don't you have a life to live?

A symphony backs up this question.

Have you been here before, and how did that work out for you?

A solo belts out these inquiries.

What I'm doing is trying to see if there's still any chance for Casey and me. I haven't lived a life since, well, since a long time ago, when I left things unfinished with her. And yes, I've been here before, but stubborn, stupid people often are the only ones who find success in this life.

I'm on the way to Savannah, and the GPS drives me out to

an exclusive neighborhood with a guard at the gate, and then perfectly cut and groomed landscapes. Yep, this is where Casey belongs. Not in the picture with me in an empty beer can of a cabin I just left back in Asheville, but with Burke in this nice new landscape.

I stop and get out at the white house with its windows and steps and pillars. I don't see any car in the driveway, so maybe that's good, or maybe it's bad. This is the address I got from an old friend of mine who knew Burke's family. But that's all I have. Just this address of the place where Burke's parents lived, the place he's been living.

Hmmm, I wonder who Casey is going to pick if she has a choice.

Maybe I shouldn't even wonder who she's going to pick. Maybe the choice was already made. Maybe I'm going to be an after-thought.

I think of the last text I sent Casey and then of trying to call her not long after that. She had changed her number and decided to shut me out for good. Which might have worked if I wasn't so dang stubborn and hardheaded.

I make it to the massive door and ring the doorbell. I wait for a couple of minutes, then ring it again.

I'm starting to head down the steps off the porch when I hear the door open like the Black Gate of Mordor. A standing hang-over stood at the door, a disheveled tornado of a man with distant eyes laced with red. He greets me with a curse and a question. I'm not exactly sure how to answer.

"I'm looking for Casey."

Maybe that's obvious, but I'm not sure if Burke knows who I am or what state he's currently residing in.

"The musician who can't sing, huh? The songwriter who can't write?"

I give him a polite nod. Years ago I would have said something comical at this, but there's nothing I can say to this now. It's the truth.

"So you come here to pee on my porch, did you? I guess I need a stray dog roaming around my place like the ones we used to have at our old mansion." He curses again and I wonder if he's going to stumble down right in front of me.

"I'm just looking for Casey."

"Well, she's not here. But I have a nice round ring that I can give you for her. You two make such a cute couple. Both of you are failures who don't know what they want. You *deserve* each other."

It's strange to see a man I've been jealous of for so many years in person standing in front of me. The backdrop of old money now simply looks old. His face looks hard, his body tired, and his eyes absent. He resembles a faded sports jersey for a player who no longer plays for the team, for a guy who didn't finish his career so well.

"Any guy would be lucky to deserve her," I tell Burke.

He just laughs and spits a big wad on the ground before him. "Ever the romantic. Yeah, try living with her. Just try it."

"If I get a chance, I will."

I think of asking where Casey is, or what she's doing, but I can't talk to this guy. I don't need him to explain anymore.

Clearly, Casey made her choice with Burke.

Clearly, the answer was no.

Daniel Suddenly Knows

"She's the One"

I GET IN MY car and smile. Then I start to laugh. Then I think for a moment and wonder if this is all a bit crazy. If this is really happening now, after all this time. But I don't hesitate. I speed down the driveway back to Asheville.

I'm not sure exactly where I need to go to find her, but I'm going to find Casey.

The countryside is passing me by and I'm speeding, not worrying about a cop stopping me. I'm cranking Springsteen's *Born to Run* and I get to track 6. The glorious track 6, which I turn up even louder.

Maybe Casey's still gone and out of my life but at least she hasn't gone back to yesterday's mistakes.

Maybe, possibly, she'll make another mistake and agree to be with me.

I'M HALFWAY TO Asheville when I hear my phone go off. I turn down the car stereo and take the call.

"Hey, man."

It's my manager, Gary.

I wouldn't have taken it if I'd known it's Gary, simply because I don't want this incredible life-affirming buzz to leave me. This sliver of hope streaking across the dark horizon of my soul. I don't need Gary to rain on my parade. I don't need the cloudy forecast I'm sure he's gonna predict.

"Hey," I say without much life in the comment.

"How's it going, buddy?"

I *especially* don't need to hear the B-word.

"What's up?"

"I gotta tell you—the new song. One word. A-M-A-Z-I-N-G."

I don't know what he's talking about. There's nothing amazing going on in my life. Well, except Casey not getting back with Burkey-boy.

"What do you mean?"

"It's great. I got it and I love it. Yeah, it's rough, but it's the best demo you guys have ever done. I love that Casey is singing it too."

Uhhhhhhh, what?

"Casey is singing? On what?"

"The demo I got a day ago. Finally listened to it."

"I didn't send you a demo."

"She did. E-mailed me it. It's great."

"You got an e-mail? A song? From Casey Sparkland?"

"Yeah, buddy. It's awesome."

I'm driving and the sun is setting and Springsteen is singing and suddenly I don't know the day or the month or the year.

"So this song—Casey's singing on it?"

"Yeah. Come on—don't act so coy. She's on the piano. I love the clever use of the word 'settle.' Awesome. 'No more pretty picture in a dress no more settling for less . . . ' I'm telling you— someone's gonna make this big. Big. *Big*."

This is all happening a bit too fast.

Thunder Road is suddenly underneath me and I'm driving at lightning speed.

"Let's talk soon, okay?" Gary says. "I've got a few ideas who I'd like to send this to."

I tell him something that resembles a "yeah, cool, sure," but I'm no longer thinking of my manager.

I'm remembering something I told Casey years ago when I decided to go off to New York to pursue my dreams.

Don't settle for less. Don't settle for second place.

All these years and she still remembers.

She still remembers.

Casey Discovers the Truth

I'VE SPENT THE last hour telling my mother what happened between Burke and me, everything from the house half belonging to me to eventually telling him I didn't want the house. Or him. Mom listens and strangely enough doesn't try to tell me what to do. Maybe she realizes by this point in life, I'm going to make my decisions on my own.

After I wait to hear something from Mom, I have to ask her what she's thinking.

"You're being *way* too quiet," I say. "You're scaring me."

"Don't be scared."

We're in the family room and are the only two in the house.

She looks at me with pretty eyes I've always felt I could never compete with. Then she wipes them and I notice there's something strange residing inside them: tears.

"I've been trying for so long to make sure you didn't experience the same thing I went through," Mom tells me. "The heartache and the sadness. Because I couldn't control my own love story—what happened with your father and I—I guess in many ways I tried to control yours. And I just . . ."

The words "I'm sorry" don't come out of her mouth. Instead, she shakes her head and tries to say something but can't. I hug her and tell her it's okay. I understand. She didn't force me to fall in love with Burke and marry him. I still made those decisions.

After a few minutes, my mother stands up and goes into the kitchen. I think she's only getting a Kleenex, but she comes back with a letter in her hand.

"I got something in the mail for you a couple days ago," Mom says. "Something I didn't want to give you."

"Why?" I ask as I take the envelope.

"A young man sent you this. I didn't open it."

I look at the front of the envelope and recognize the handwriting. Then I see the name at the corner:

Daniel Winter.

I hold the letter in my hand, a bit afraid to open it, not sure what he wants or needs to say.

"There's one more thing," Mom says, giving me a tender smile

I haven't seen in a very long time. "This same young man called while you were out with your sister for dinner."

"What did you say to him?"

"I just told him you'd be back later this evening."

I can't help but smile, knowing God had heard those prayers of mine.

I just never thought He'd act so fast.

Daniel Finds His Secret Garden

I WANT TO RUN over to her house, but I realize I need to clean myself up a bit. I need to stop home and get my bearings and maybe make something out of the nest of hair on my head. Maybe put some nicer clothes on. I was clothed in desperation when I went over to Burke's mansion. I need to change and put on a little confidence.

The pit stop at my father's takes longer than I want it to, since I have to feed him dinner and remind him I'm not the tax guy named Bobby who cheated him out of $1,000 years ago. But it's okay. I can be patient. Sorta.

Thirty-five years I've waited for this moment. For this emotion. For this moonlit night.

Thirty-five years I've waited for her.

I've been looking and longing for the perfect song for my entire life. I just never realized it was always there, right in plain view, for everybody to see and hear.

I finally get in my car after the sun has disappeared, and I can feel my hands and the rest of my body shake. I'm so happy, and yet still so unsure, and I'm still very much like that eighteen-year-old kid driving around wondering and hoping and trying to figure out just what to do.

I don't think adults figure it out. They just get better at faking it. They get used to feigning wisdom.

I'm about ready to turn on the radio, but I don't. I just drive. I don't need a song to drive to. I already have the song inside my head. I know the melody by heart. And I finally, after tonight, have heard the lyrics.

They were a long time coming. A very long time coming.

I slow down. Stop. Turn. Drive. Slow, stop, turn.

Then I find myself on her street again. I slow the car down and I roll my window down. In my dreams I've driven down here and found her waiting. Just like now. Just like this moment, as I look up and see that familiar figure sitting on the rooftop, as if she's been waiting for me her whole life.

I get the chills.

I hope to God that this isn't a dream, because I don't want to wake up if it is.

I flicker my headlights so she knows I'm coming. I see a hand wave like it did so many years ago and I have to laugh. So ridiculous. We're two schoolchildren here again. We've gone so far only to come back around to here. To now. To her rooftop.

I get out of the car and stand and stare up at her house. Then I realize the car is still running.

I can see Casey looking at me and smiling at me. I can't tell if she has tears in her eyes, but I think she does.

I love you and this time you're not getting away from me.

I walk toward the edge of the house she is sitting by.

For a moment, I'm just standing below her, standing and staring and smiling, looking at this girl I never wanted to leave. We're just looking at each other and waiting.

"Nice night to look at the stars," I tell her.

"I came up here to study my memories. They're painted all over the sky."

"Memories in the stars?" I ask, thinking about telling her that so long ago. "Whoever thought of that must be really smart."

"Oh, I don't know about that. But he is very special."

"Can he climb up there and sit next to you?"

"I was hoping to make another memory tonight."

Settle Yourself

*T*HESE STARS STILL feel so close and so warm. Like a field of sunflowers I can fall into. I sit on my mother's rooftop one more time, remembering lying there still hoping and still believing. I feel heavy, but not because of all the unfulfilled dreams weighing me down, but because of the hardened heart that has filled their place. I want to believe you don't have to be a twenty-something to start over again, and that maybe, possibly, life is all about starting over again, day after day after day.

It's not a surprise when Daniel shows up. Burke called me earlier to curse and yell at me in a voice mail. At least he warned me about Daniel looking for me. It allowed me to get out of my sweats and do something with myself. Not that I feel I have to. Not with the man climbing up the tree to sit on the roof next to me.

It's strange to see him sitting next to me. For a moment, we just sit next to each other in silence. Then I hear him laugh.

"You know that years ago, I did the same thing?" Daniel finally says.

"Climbing up on my roof in the middle of the night?"

He shakes his head. All this time and all these years and he still looks the same. Daniel Winter will always look the same.

"Praying for a miracle," he tells me. "Once again, God answered it."

"I should have waited. I should have stayed, Daniel. I should have remained by your side in college."

"You're still here."

"You know what I mean."

I feel him take my hand. "I've had my chances. We've had our chances."

"Do you believe there are more than just second chances?"

He laughs. "Every day I'm given another one, Casey."

Suddenly I start crying. I cry for a while and rest my head against his shoulder.

"I feel so old, yet I don't have anything to show for it," I tell him.

"You have me. Me and my rusted-out heart. A hollow heart that still loves you."

"Hey," I say, sitting back up and looking at him. "That was a pretty good line."

"I always have them when I'm around you. Because they're not lines. They're just thoughts I'm thinking."

"Daniel—I don't know—"

"And I don't either," he interrupts. "Listen, I'm here. And I'm holding your hand. And I'm gazing at you under the stars. And I'm not asking for anything except for you to stay by my side for a while. That's all I want. Just to know you're there. Right now."

I feel my body shake, and Daniel could feel it too, so he puts his arm around me.

So many years and here we were once again.

"This is like some country song," I say. "*We're* like some country song."

"No, we're not. There's usually never any resolution in those. Just heartache and longing."

"We've had both."

"Then maybe it's time to stop the track and create a new song. An entirely different one."

I can see the shadow of his face glancing my way. He looks older. Not the way he appears, but the way he's talking and carrying himself. That youthful fearlessness is no longer there.

"I love you, Casey Sparkland," Daniel says, interrupting my thoughts. "But it's not the breathless kind of passionate love that comes when you're standing near me, the kind that makes me want to lose myself and leave everything behind. It's the kind that stays with me, night after night, reminding me what I once had, reminding me what I *did* leave behind. That kind of love—that's the kind of love it's grown into. The kind that men like me—"

"Just shut up," I say softly, my voice choked. "Shut up and kiss me."

"Are you asking?"

"No. Not this time."

I feel his lips against my cheek, kissing the tears that have streamed down. Then I find myself kissing another chance and another opportunity and another gift in my grace-filled life.

I kiss tomorrow even as yesterday holds me in his arms.

It's a beautiful place to be.

It's a silent place full of unspoken songs and unheard melodies.

If youth is wasted on the young
Then let's be two old souls
Together saving the moments
Together patching the holes.
—Sparkland & Winter, "Settle Yourself"

Epilogue

*T*HE MOMENT I see her walk into full view, the world
seems to stop. Casey Sparkland lives up to her name, in a
white glowing bridal gown with a long train and short modern veil
draped over her face. I see her smile at me while a couple hundred
spectators smile at her. She pauses, then takes her father's arm and
begins to walk down the aisle as the music plays.

She's walking toward me. After all these years, she's finally
gonna be mine.

It's been almost a year since last summer, since I came back
home and found her waiting on her roof. We've taken things
slowly—as slowly as two souls in our shoes could take things. But

eventually we planned it all out to happen in the middle of June. Every little detail has been decided together—from the type of wedding cake to where we'd be going on our honeymoon—but really, all that matters is this moment.

Casey's smile. The realization that my persistence mattered. The surprise that her love lasted.

As she nears and the faces of our guests turn, I see her mother. We've made our peace, even though I still know she wants someone more reliable than a musician. I see the tears on Casey's mother's face and know she's happy for her.

When I touch Casey's soft hand, I have to remind myself where we are again. I know the church and the people around us, but I forget where we are in time. Did we just graduate college, starting a life together? Could it be that some evil soul pressed the Pause button for so long?

It doesn't matter. She's here and you're here and you both are about to make that big declaration.

I see that cute little face of hers. So grown-up and so beautiful, but still forever that spunky Casey I met in high school years ago. She gives me a look I'll forever be able to write songs about.

I've been looking and longing for the perfect song for my entire life. I just never realized it was always there, right in plain view, for everybody to see and hear.

"Hey, handsome," Casey says to me as we stand side by side in front of the pastor.

"Hey, beautiful."

Our smiles don't leave our mouths, and our glances don't leave each other. We say our vows and light the candles and listen to the songs played. Then the preacher tells me to say "I do" and tells Casey to say it too.

Finally, we're at that moment we've been preparing for half our lives. This beautiful moment when I lift that veil and see her pretty smile.

I know Casey can read my mind, but I say it anyway.

"Are you gonna kiss me or not?"

I plan to keep asking her this. For the rest of our lives.